# The Silent Betrayal

## By

## Momus Najmi

*Dedicated to my loving wife – there is nothing more precious in my life than you.*

Devoid of any natural sustenance of sense in the most common of forms, this man has come to a point where nature predicted it to be, a point of extinction. But now that I face the last choice to be made, of whether to jump in or fly out, I have managed to grow a conscience, one of the most inconvenient sorts. As I see it there is a time to die and a time to kill oneself. I wish not to indulge in any of those appealing to the forgotten senses. I died the day I started living and I killed myself the moment I realized my existence.

"Are you going to finish that?" A very good question, am I going to finish my scotch or will it finish me? Don't worry; this is not the diary of an alcoholic. It's just that I have been annoyingly holding this glass of wondrous delight for far too long without even taking a sip. I don't even remember when my secretary led this buffoon to my office, come to think of it I don't know why my secretary is working so late I told her to go home ages ago.

"An apt question my dear friend, if I may be bold enough to call you my friend. Will I finish it? Will I finish the first glass and pour a second and carry on the cycle of drinking so you don't feel awkward polishing this vintage liquor all by yourself? A very fine question indeed. To tell you the truth, and this is with the deepest respect, go fuck yourself."

Now you would think that he is going to get up and punch the smug off my face, I would expect that too in most circumstances but maybe only in those that had me saying those very words without the influential protection of my bank account and this sturdy dividing desk. He is getting up and he is most certainly fucking off, so don't you fret I will live for a few more pages still. But this is exactly what I am talking about, my conscience is being very inconvenient. I just lost a multi-billion dollar deal with my fiercest business rival. I suppose there are billions more that can be made. I am not really sure how many billions to be honest, if I said multimillion would it make it more believable to you? But obviously it matters not; it is what I say it to be.

I am to be married within a year, to someone whose name is still not embedded in my memory as my father would like it to be. And the night just after this sudden to me yet expected from all others morally decapitating news, I have been given the task to seal the deal of a business acquisition that even the devil would fret to conjure. The deal with her father's company, there is to be a merger after our marriage.

"Your actions are most discerning, and no you may not call me your friend, you are not even worthy of being an enemy. Many congratulations for your forthcoming wedding, I hope the bride brings some well needed sense in you." He puts the glass down on the side table by the door, thank heavens for a minute I thought he would actually take it, I like that glass. I never wanted the deal to go through, their finances never matched and their dealings with the government were nothing less than shady. But I suspect this deal will go through no matter what I do, there might be much more I can do then just pissing off their chief negotiator – I shouldn't doubt my abilities.

"Thank you, my no one," I say with the utmost courteous spite, he looks at me for one last time with a hint of anticipation that it might be all a youthful frivolity played out by me. He shakes his head and mutters as he leaves, "The pleasure was all mine."

I guess dad would not be pleased to know what I have just done. My loyalty has already grown doubtful with him and so has his credibility to me. Sometimes in life, you need to ask the questions and expect some answers back. I do not wish to be married to this woman and I do not wish to be a part of this company any more. But there are a lot more people than myself, a lot more happier possibilities than mine that would be affected if I chose to be selfish. Perhaps I just need to figure out a way to expose his lies and dark past, and take control of the company. I can do so much good with it.

"Why did you do that?" It's barely morning and I have not even opened my eyes properly and there he is howling down on me. The smell of oak flowing through him, those stubby fingers opening the curtains and letting the severity of Ra pour over me.

"For God's sake, leave me alone." I cry out resembling an eleven year old that persists not to leave me and stay forgotten inside me.

"If God had any say in this world I would not be alive now and you would be even more spoiled than you already are, why did you do that Johann?" He comes closer to me, seems he hasn't slept all night, his eyes look weary and he has more wrinkles than before.

"It didn't feel like the right thing to do."

"Feel you say Master Johann, so have we started feeling again now? I must say it's the most inconvenient of times to be feeling things now." He drags a chair and sits by my side, examining me, waiting for me to say to him, what I had wanted to for a couple of weeks now. He knows there is something going on in my head, but he will not ask of me till I tell him of my free will. He said nothing when my father announced the plans for my marriage to a beautiful yet a deceptively purposeful woman. He said nothing, when I told him the reason behind it. And now he is sitting here, waiting for me to tell him.

"Gilby, for some reason it didn't seem at all important to me last night. And to be honest their company is even more crooked than ours. But he reminded me of my imminent doom and then nothing felt important to me. All I kept thinking was about that girl I saw at the charity event few weeks ago. I cannot get her out of my head." I feel a bit childish saying it, but I know I can tell Gilbert anything and he would understand. Gilbert Pohl has been with me for as long as I remember, for me he is a substitute father or a closest thing to a friend, in reality he is my butler – my half German, half English butler.

"Is it wise to think about other girls, a day after agreeing to a proposal of marriage?" He is doing it again, arguing for the sake of argument. He wants me to be sure of what I intend to do or what I might intend to do. I do not know my own intentions yet, all I know is I have this sudden desire for the first time in my life to explore my intentions, should I give them up so easily? "Is it wise to have lived and keep on living this life of leisure and be limited to your wants?" He gives a sigh; do not really know if he even thinks anything of my desire to explore right now. He has something of his own on his mind and wants me to get on with the day. But if that was entirely true he wouldn't have bothered poking my mind like that. Gilbert has his secrets, I know he does, but I feel his secrets have started growing secrets of their own now.

"Well then a rebel must do what a rebel must do. But I would advise you not to give such reasons to your father. His wants exceed the wants of others. Now freshen up, and have your

breakfast before you start getting howled at by that beast."
My father is worse than a beast, we both know it although
we do not know his specific kind of beast, so should we
condemn him to hate? Yes, definitely.

"Gilby, he is my father." I look at him trying to see beyond
that face hiding my smirk as best I can. There is so little he
lets on, what is it that he sees outside my window? I know
my father must be sitting in the garden having his tea waiting
for me to come down so he can humiliate me in the
openness of the sky, under the sun on such a beautiful day.
But what does Gilbert see outside? A distant memory, is it a
good one or a bad one? Or one that alters another memory?
"Lest you forget, young master."

---

I feel like I have not washed my face for ages, the cold water
splashing on my face seems like a memory of yester years.
My skin is drinking the water, eager to refresh itself. My face
looks a bit rugged as well, let's give it a good shave. I have
never been able to understand this whole concept of hair,
especially on the face, forming a beard. What is a beard
really if not unwanted facial pubes? They grow back so
quickly and then we have to go through this whole ritual of
shaving cream, razor blade, ouch ouch I cut myself, wash the
face, and put the aftershave on, Oww that burns and back
again looking like a human being but knowing this cycle will
repeat itself in the very near future. Ridiculous and

interesting at the same time, more appealing than the old fart waiting for me downstairs.

It is such a beautiful day outside; my mother chose this room for me a long time ago because of the view. Acres and acres of land and forest can be seen from here, all owned by our family. Mum and I used to spend hours in our garden and every now and then go for a long walk in to the forest along the stream soaking up our tired feet. The days of youthful innocence, things used to be so different back then. I never managed to form a good relationship with my father, just the occasional hello and goodnight, now he doesn't even bother saying hello. There had never been a reason to talk with him, and the more I got to know him the more I understood his devious mind. I could see my mother never really loved him, but she never complained about him to me, that was her nature. He did not even attend her funeral, he was on a business trip when she passed away, said it was pointless now that she was already dead.

For days I stayed in my room, grieving by myself, with Gilby forcing me to take care of myself, comforting me, being a father I never had. For days I looked out of this window, expecting her to just come back from one of her strolls, or just sitting there in the garden having her tea, reading one of her silly romantic novels. She was the only person who although never understood me but never judged me for the way I was, always encouraged me to be the best I could be. And now every morning that I look out of the window, I see him, the stone marauder, makes me want to bar this window.

Ah my breakfast, I see Gilbert has not devoid me of bacon today, eggs, his special sweet aromatic bread and a glass of freshly made orange juice. You know there is nothing in this world I hate more than a pulp ridden orange juice but I do not have the heart to tell him that, I always drink it like a medicine. He hasn't given me the newspaper today that's a change. Knowing what has been going wrong in the world never sets you in a good mood in the morning anyway. But he has given me something to read, how delightful, a short story and he has written over the top of the front page, 'the story is about a tomato trying to escape a farm', amusingly innocent. It is by one of the kids from the orphanage we fund, Klaudia's Home for Children, I named it after my mother. We suggested the teachers to have a competition every month for best story writing to encourage children to love literature and embrace creativity. My mother wanted me to be a writer, I always loved literature but I was never a good writer, to be honest I never tried. But she always encouraged me, told me there is a masterpiece in all of us. Every month they send us stories and we choose one, and put a special extra in their individual college fund.

"Did you choose this story than, Gilbert? It is a good story." Gilbert starts straightening up my bed without even looking at me. "No, this is the only one that was sent to us this time."

"That's strange!" I can sense he is annoyed about something, and I can guess what that something might be, but assumptions are always misleading.

"No, what is more strange is me choosing a story every month, going through all those wonderful stories that are actually meant to be read by you. They put in a lot of effort to write these stories, the least you can do is read them." He seems a bit angrier than usual, has something happened I wonder? If something has happened I am sure this is not what has annoyed him, he is only hiding behind it.

"Is everything alright, Gilbert?" I ask without hope, for I know the answer to it – but yet again I do not like making assumptions.

"Everything is fine Johann, I just feel like you have forgotten all what your mother stood for and cared for. I do not want you to turn into someone your mother will be ashamed to call her son." Harsh but honest.

"Not now Gilby, I have enough perplexities to deal with today as it is." I look at him hoping he breaks and lets it out. What is it that's actually bothering you old friend?

"I am sorry, young master." He says it but obviously doesn't mean it. He lets out half a smile as he is going about cleaning my room which is already very tidy and clean, it is a sad smile – remembering a distant memory. He knows what I am going to ask of him next, he usually gets what he wants – I am glad he does, what would I be without him? Another money grubbing monster waiting in the garden to humiliate his only son.

"Apology accepted, now can you make the arrangements so we can visit the kids and rejuvenate their love for the written word as soon as I am done with my father today?" I know I am avoiding the issue, but sometimes you have to avoid the issue temporarily to try and understand it fully.

"Today is not a very good day for that I think." For deserted Christ's sake, what does he want? Does he want me to go or what?

"Gilbert ..."

"There is a charity fund-raiser that I think you should really attend today. It is for the kids in Africa, who have lost their parents or otherwise left disabled because of all the horrors of illegal diamond mining." He looks at me with all the innocence of a wilder beast trying but failing to be mysteriously mischievous.

"That is a very specific fund-raiser." Diamond mining, why do I feel I will end up mining the secrets I need not to at this fund-raiser?

"Well it is not really just for that, but that is a major part of it. I think you should really go. I know Blakemore Industries stopped dealing with diamonds a long time ago but I think our involvement of late in this industry can be looked upon positively if we contribute with our support for them."

"Very well, Gilbert, very well. I shall do as my Lord commands." You were never the one for business development and company image; I know this is not what is in your mind but what the hell lets go with it.

"Let it go will you, okay I think you should go now to him. Good luck." I do not need luck and just a bit of patience to deal with that dying Cretan.

"Good morning father." I try to greet him with the least bit of venom as I make my way to the grand tree where he is sat upon his chair, drinking whiskey and smoking cigar in the sun. Such a waste of the sun, and good taste, he drinks whiskey when wine blossoms in his reach, fool that he is, drunk before the day even starts.

"And what is so marvellously good about this morning. May I ask my only son whose stupidity precedes his very presence?" He looks at me momentarily and returns back to gazing wildly in the distance, towards the forest where shadows lurk and his sight follows them not.

"Only that you are alive and I am about to commit to death, my dear father." I sit myself down beside him, while someone comes in out of the numerous servants we employ to fill my glass with the most reddest of wines. What life do we provide them? Spending entire life waiting on a person like me, whose making has been in more rigorous complexities than the wine they pour yet doesn't even come close to the hardship from which the sweet taste nourishingly sprouts.

"So you have come to your senses? She is the most beautiful and most intelligent of all girls you have come across, I do not know why you complain. Men drool at the sight of her, everyone wants to make her theirs but you is all she wants." He lets a big puff of smoke gently escape his eroding mouth, more interested in starring at the interweaving of the airy particles than me. Is he not even going to talk about the deal that I broke yesterday, or tried to break.

"That is the bit that disturbs me most." I say while still trying to catch his eye.

"Be grateful, are you afraid to fuck her? Have your balls gone dry sleeping with all those whores?" So classy, my father.

"Unless you gave those girls gonorrhoea first, I think everything is fine down there. It is something that you would not understand and which doesn't matter anyway." I wish I had it in me just to badger his face against that damn tree repeatedly till his blood would bring a new shade of colour to it than have a conversation with him.

He finally looks at me, maybe that last bit unnerved him a little. Did he actually believe I wouldn't notice the plethora of young girls that walk through our halls into his chamber? Our house, if I can call it that. It might be big, but not big enough for such prime voluptuous asses to go by unnoticed. "It is something that I do not want to understand. You are lucky I am not having your head chopped off for trying to break that deal yesterday. One thing I entrusted you with and you screw it up. So be useful to me for once in your damned life and go ahead with this marriage." Finally, but is that all. It was a multi-billion deal, a prelude to this proposed marriage. I wouldn't let anyone make such a decision on a feeling of ill-trust. What is he not revealing to me? Is this marriage that important to him? Something doesn't seem very right, but surely having this constipated face of misguided concentration is not going to help right now.

"I shall try my best not to disappoint you, father." I say with a smirk which by some luck he ignores completely.

"Good now here she comes, try to be a bit amiable towards her." I don't even know her you stupid old git, how can I be amiable towards her, you medieval contemplation of a rotting innate reflex.

"Yes I will be." What else can I say?

"Now you know of her as Gladys, but her actual name in Galadriel. Just call her Gladys, why the fuck did I tell you that, you are way too immature for such information." Instead of a Dark Lord, you would have a queen, not dark but beautiful and terrible as the dawn. Tempestuous as the sea, and stronger than the foundations of the earth. All shall love me and despair.

"Are you serious?"  What has my life come to? I am to be married with Galadriel, how did she even survive her childhood. I mean, it is a nice name, but not the one you want to marry. What am I going to call her? Galadriel dear, can you stop with that bowl of future rendering horror provoking water and come back to bed?

"Good morning father." My father gets up to greet her, and hugs her. He got up to greet her, he wouldn't even look at me when on various unfortunate moments I have to sit down with him. But then she is Galadriel, you would stand up in her presence, the mighty elf queen.

"Good morning sweetheart." Sweetheart, really? What is that old oaf planning? And he is smiling, oh my lord, the wind must have committed suicide after touching the crookedness of his face. "I have to go attend some business, rectify few mistakes," he says as he throws a quick glance at me. I do not even prefer the back of his head than his face; I just wish he drops dead on his way.

Now that Galadriel has sat herself down, I look at her. She does glow of beauty but utter and deep annoyance as well. "Since when have you been calling my father as father?" It a very legitimate question, even a dying orphan riddled with disease and hunger adopted by him would not call him father, I only call him out of spite.

"Since we were paired to be married my dear Johann." Why must you persist to be this annoying?

"Can we cut this dear crap please?" My mother used to call me that; I shall not let her call me like such.

"Of course my love."

"Arghh!"I give up.

"I know you are not fond of me much, and I want you to know that I am not forcing you into this. We have to do this for the good of all but it doesn't mean we have to be miserable and be like one of those couples who never talk to each other and have separate bedrooms." Her grace affords me with wisdom.

"I didn't know that was still in fashion, might give it a shot." I am not having it you elf bitch.

"Johann ..."

I interrupt her, "All right Lady Galadriel, please excuse my insolence, I seek not but your forgiveness."

"Very funny! Just call me Gladys please." She looks annoyed, maybe now she feels what I feel. "It is quite funny actually my dearest elven queen." She is boiling, "Can you please ....."

"You are wise and fearless and fair, Lady Galadriel. I will give you the One Ring, if you ask for it. It is too great a matter for me." I am bursting of joyous eruptions inside, I feel like a kid bullying a nerd but to be honest in a very nerdy way.

"I do not want your bloody ring." If she gets angrier I fear her tits are going to be on fire.

"Then what do you wish?" I cannot help it but to carry on this jibe.

"That what should be shall be." We both burst out laughing. I was not expecting that. "It is not my fault that my father was a Tolkien fan, it is not that bad of a name. Can you just please call me Gladys instead."

We smile in silence for a while, trying to sink in the after effects of that light hearted moment we just shared. "Johann please, at least try to know me before you start hating me."

She is right, I do not even know her and yet I am affording so much hatred towards her. It is the principle of it that I abhor more than the person. "Okay but what about you, why do you love me so much without knowing me?"

"Who said I loved you? I am just trying to be polite." Our feelings seem similar but yet so different at the same time.

"Okay fine, I get the drift. I am sorry. I didn't mean to be like … I mean I am not usually .. you know." I relinquish my hold for the moment.

"Yes I know." She says with a genuine smile, so rare these days. But why are we doing this? Why am I doing this? I ask myself as I have on so many other occasions. I do not know the why of my doings yet I do them. I feel like a monk or a priest, lost in the in-between never knowing the why but forever following the pink elephant.

"Would you like to come to a charity fund-raiser with me tonight?" I feel sorry for her; it is not entirely her fault.

"I didn't know you were into charity as such." It is one of the many things I am 'into' like hacking the heads of new-borns, slow cooking pandas to a delicious smouldering stew, sun-bathing naked in front of the little girls' schools, you name it I am into it. You know what I mean, what else am I to do? A rich bastard with more than he deserves, give a penny from a million back and they love you as a saviour with a compassionate heart.

"Well it will be a chance for us to get to know each other better, so what do you say?" Why must I simply yield to my father and do as he say? And why must I even try to like her. And why am I inviting her to the charity fund-raiser?

"Of course." Of course you would say of course. I am sure she doesn't have that many unlikeable traits, at least not by the looks of it. I mean, if I were to abode inside my trousers like most men, I wouldn't think twice but have her as a life-long companion. There is no mystery, I might find surprises tucked deep in her cupboard as we go along but it still would not be a surprise. Because I know who I am going to be with and from whom those surprises will come. And that knowing to me should be followed by a feeling of excruciating agony, for being around the person constantly would result in my dim mind formulating familiarity as love or all-consuming hatred. This feels like I am being led to a lifelong of rape convention by, let's be honest an amazingly well shape arsed girl, but still the word predominant in that sentence is rape and not the beautiful ass she possess. Forceful pleasure. Being forced to enjoy something or someone in this case so divine which you would have rather wanted to enjoy by your own device, through your own means and probably with a different divinity altogether to give yourself that feeling of accomplishment.  This might be a more relaxed version of arranged marriage but it is still an arranged marriage – a life time of mental and physical rape for both me and her alike.

"I will pick you up at 7." I say after quite a substantial pause. I do not really remember for how long my thoughts were rambling on for.

"I cannot wait." She smiled, a different more pretend one, gave me a quick peck on my cheek and left in a rather springy posture than the sturdiness she came with. Okay perhaps referring this to rape is a bit of an exaggeration.

"You do not need to go through all of that, I have already picked appropriate attire for you tonight." Obviously you have, and chosen an appropriate moment to disturb my chain of thoughts. He somehow always knows when my mind is spinning out of control.

"I just want to pick something out for myself, something that is more me." I am holding an orange polka dotted shirt; I admit I wasn't really paying attention to what I was doing. His reactions were strange today, there is something my devious father is hiding from me, something big, something monumental. I already know there is something wrong, but it seems the something wrong I know a bit about and trying to find out more about is leading to something terribly wrong before I even have time to catch up to the something wrong.

"Are you sure about taking her with you tonight?" Would you rather have me take Minnie mouse in a tramp suit? My mind is ravaging, I need to know, I hate being in the unknown.

Gilbert is looking at me now with his curious yet cautious stare. He knows there is something building up, I need a neutralizing thought. "Yes, well we need to start getting along; this will just give me a chance to know her better." Oh yes, rebel turning soft approach, might not work permanently but defuse the situation for the time being. I need more time to think about this, I need to know but I cannot have him knowing at least not yet.

"We both know that you are going to be too distracted to pay any attention to her." You are too smart for it my friend, well I am sorry but I have keep on playing this game with you. Even I do not know what I am thinking right now, I cannot tell you I have suspicions about my father. I do not have anything to base it on, just a reaction that might as well have been because of his age, and obviously an approach by CIA to look into his past. Something to do with him going to doctor so much lately. Maybe he has cancer, one can only hope.

"That is the plan." I say with my usual smirk.

He lets out a long sigh, he knows I am not going to tell him what is actually going on but he is not going to push on, "If you are going to give it a go, why not just give it a go then?"

Give it a go, maybe I will. I do not really have that much to lose. Never been able to form any meaningful relationship with anyone, maybe this is the only way rich demented people like me can have an outwardly happy seeming family life. Much like my father, my mind is seriously spinning out of control. "I do not like doing straight forward things my friend, I will eventually sit down and know her properly but not before I have had my fun."

"Okay, do it your way, as long as you are doing it." He starts going through my other wardrobe, the sensible clothes wardrobe. Wait I thought he had coffee for me, I asked for it ages ago.

"I thought you were going to get me coffee, Gilby?" He doesn't seem to have heard it.

"Just pick out something more sensible then that shirt you have in your hand." Okay he didn't hear, or just ignored. I guess I am not having my coffee any time soon. "How about this? This looks perfect," I say with every inch of innocence I could muster.

He just looks at me with a point blank expression, I don't blame him, "It's yellow, it is a yellow suit. You want to go to a charity event with your future wife dressed like Big Bird?"

I do like yellow, "That Bird has made this colour a disaster for everyone."

"Yellow was never been in fashion for formal occasions as far as I can remember. Before you pick out a pink suit or a bright blue suit with glowing Christmas lights running through it might I suggest you just go with my choice?" He is still annoyed with me for not telling him the thing that has been bugging me for months now and which has taken paramount buggingness level as of today.

I am not going to give up that easily, I can pick my clothes, "Hold on! How about that black suit? The one that I got made last year, that fit me quite well, I looked so sophisticated in it, you said it yourself."

"Yes, till I looked at the back of it, 'Metal Rules' with an obscene hand gesture." To be honest it is not much of a suit when you wear it with all its gear but it looks the deal. "Oh yeah! Metal does rule," I feel like a teenager again saying that, the freedom of thoughts I had back then, be able to do so many things that a successful business man cannot do.

"Perhaps it does sir, but I firmly believe that even Robb Flynn would not wear such a thing to a charity fund-raiser." Do not let it fool you; he has been to every Machine Head gig I have been to. It might be because I told him to accompany me, but I saw him nodding his head about when he thought I wasn't looking with his leg flapping about like a drummer who has been tied down and made to listen to pure metal, but obviously he is right about the suit thing.

"All right, so what has Gucci Gilby picked out for me? Let's see." I cannot play this game for long, normally I would go on for hours being a nuisance but I just want to get on with it.

"It's a simple suit, it neither shouts out you are too damn rich for your own good nor that you are sleeping on the streets." It is the same suit I wore on my mother's death anniversary this year with the exception of the tie, is that really appropriate right now. I didn't go anywhere, I was supposed to go to the orphanage and meet the kids, remember her through her good work. Instead I just wore the suit, went into the forest, and got drunk – usual tradition. He is putting my mother issue too strongly on me as of lately. "I am quite impressed, especially with the tie. I thought you hated red ties."

"Yes but Gladys is wearing red and its appropriate for you to match on some basis." When did she have time to tell you that? Did she already know I was going to invite her? Wait no that is quite an absurd thought. She probably just likes red, interesting thing to know about her.

"You are being quite Mr Fashion today aren't you, my devilish match maker." I do not know if he is doing it because he likes her or because he thinks it will do me good. We both really need to sit down and compare notes, it's getting quite frustrating.

"We wouldn't have to do this, if you were a normal billionaire and had a stylist and a personal tailor to do this for you. I suggested Fabiani to you, he is the best around."

"But he likes touching my balls too much, Gilby."

"Just shut it and get ready please, it's getting late."

A black envelope, I cannot stop thinking about it. Can it really be true? I do not put it past my father to have done something of a momentous criminal kind but the CIA sending black envelopes to me is a thing unknown. This is the fifth letter I have received in as little as a month, all letters say the same thing, 'For the good of his keep a boy must become a man and wash away the sins of his father'. I know very dramatic, I am told they like such sort of nonsense.

My father funded the last presidential campaign, his choice lost although it came very close. Republicans do really know how to pick amazingly nasty characters. I showed my support for the Democrats, I am sure you must have heard of it. The split in the house of Blakemore, one way or another they will get their man in White House. There was a lot of talk about it. To be honest I had only done it to oppose my father, and because I had the necessary funds to do it. He turned it into a publicity stunt at the end, claiming that Blakemore Industries is the most liberal company in America, and feels strongest for the future of its country that it refuses to blindly follow without knowing. I do not know whatever that was supposed to mean, but people thought we allow open mindedness and debate within our company – they still think that – and that we actually do care for the future of the country, utter bullshit.

Anyway my point was, during the campaign, which I only gave money towards and few interviews and not much, I met a CIA, what should I call, representative let's say. He told me, time will come when my country would need me in earnest and then I shall be delivered a letter in black. I know seriously they are always this dramatic, mad crazy for it. And so I have, five times now, and five times have I ignored it. Four times I have ignored it, I have not decided upon the fifth time yet.

I do not really know what they want of him and why they don't approach him directly. I know somehow he is to blame for my mother's death. I do not remember much of that day, all I remember is going to the lake with my mother and then being carried back to the mansion by Gilbert, too late to save us both. My treacherous father must have had something to do with it, Olympian swimmers don't just drown in lakes for no reason. Maybe she figured out his whatever dark secrets, and perhaps that is why CIA is trying to reach out to me. He killed her, I know he did. The black letter will be answered if only black death can be his fate.

I have a bit of an idea that the company is not completely clean, then again no company in this world is truly clean. But trying to find out few things I have uncovered something disturbing and I do not really know what to make of it at this point. I still don't see the connection with intelligence agencies; this unknown is purely financial matter. Perhaps they believe my father is going to die soon, one can only hope, and they know about the divide between us two. Making some sort of suspicious past, giving me a purpose to overthrow him and take control, and them lending me a hand in achieving all this – that would make me appreciate their help and be in their debt. A long game – but long games are their speciality. Whatever it is, it will have to wait. I have got a date to go to.

---

As I go towards the garage to figure out which vehicle would be best suited for my grand pursuit tonight I pass my father, sitting solemnly in the study with a drink in one hand and a letter in the other. He has been drinking a lot more than usual these days, not that I am concerned about his health; it's just that he never does things out of the usual. He is very religious about his routine and expects everyone else to have a rigorous one as well. If I can remember he always used to say that if you are not bound by your routine than you are bound by an illness of mind which comes about by thinking of thoughts which are unknown to your thinking. A letter, he is holding a letter and that also personally written, on a paper that looks more yellow than his teeth.  What is haunting him so much? I see a shadow fall over the half open door; a hand reaches out and rests on the side of the door.

"Johann, can I help you or do you want to speak with your father?" A disgusting and unsavoury smile befits the face of this loathsome character, Simon, or slime-one as I call him inside my head. My father's number one – whatever that means – I have known him longer than well my dead mother. Known him, that is a very broad term, known of him to be exact. He brings up such hatefulness in me, one of these days I am going to snap and I will kill him – very slowly.

"No just checking if he is dead yet or not."

"We can't all be that lucky son." The unmistakable voice of my hateful father yells out from behind the door. "Close the door, Simon." Not today, I need to put my charity face on.

---

I don't think so we need to go on about my hundreds of cars, monstrous trucks, motorbikes and the choice that I had to make, and the interweaving pathways I had to take to get to her house, if you can call that a house. I thought our mansion was extravagant, but this looks like a castle with a whole village inside, except there are no people and it is not really a castle. There is so much speculation about our business dealings going on and the known wealth and so on, it is a wonder why I elect to go all alone on my own without any guards or any form of security. It might be because I wish to be independent, or maybe because I like rediscovering myself especially on these pages all to the more annoyance to myself and you alike. And there she is my beautiful bride to be, so remarkable and so stunning, but a forced beauty on this disgruntled beast.

"I thought you'd never come, my Johann." That is a bit unfair I am only late by three minutes. She gives me a kiss, a slight long held intimate one on my lips and I return her the favour. Oddly enough this is our first kiss, how unromantic and casual; we will have a hell of a mundane time together. "See, that wasn't that scary, now was it?" No, it wasn't scary but unexpected. If I were to look through my hormonal composition rather than the rational construction of my mind I have to say, she has got a body to die for. The dress or any thread woven delight for that matter sits on her so comfortably running through her luscious curves enjoying the slimness of her wonderment, revealing yet not revealing enough, tempting every particle in me to explore her beauty with adoring tenderness yet ravenous desire than it is intended to be.

"I hope you are not planning on eating me tonight," she giggles, sweet giggling, "Stop it, you are making me blush. Stop looking at me like that." I am not looking, I am drooling. There is a difference. Come back to your senses. What is wrong with me? Only few hours ago I was impartial of our union and now my pants are ready to explode. This is most unusual. Lust, pure lust, I know it might sound strange but I am not used to that emotion – if you can call it that. You might find it bemusing, but to me it hinders mental progress as is displayed right now by my dumbfounded face. These emotions need to be explored, but I have to say something first before it gets too awkward.

"I apologize for making you uncomfortable, it wasn't my intent, believe me. You look very beautiful in that dress, it suits you." Do not really care what I say right now, I just want her to be all right with it so we can proceed with my thoughts. "It is fine, you don't need to apologize. You are only human." Cliché is as cliché does. "Now come on or we will be late."

Okay, I think that was adequately dealt with. I have not scared her and further more established a contact of flirtation so let's move on. Lust, yes I have not felt lust in such a way before. Well, I have but that is only childish lust, horny teenager syndrome, which doesn't mean anything or count for anything since you are still trying to discover the enigma of hard malignant giganotosaurus and the means to relinquish the throb – anything would do, and the lust within those paradigms as usually defined is temporary. I have never bothered looking into it within myself in detail; it is probably heat of the moment, the sooner gone the better I can spend my time on more meaningful endeavours. This is a more, if it can be said over here, mature form of that same emotion, enhanced and not in the most comfortable of ways. I clearly would not be shy of exploring it with a practical application on penalty of losing the respect of my person for life but on the same hand there is an uneasiness that is creeping inside with the thought of such explorations. It surely isn't love, whatever it is, as far as I know about love it isn't finding satisfaction in the greatness of fuck, no matter how amazing it maybe, it is about finding satisfaction in everything apart from that. Look at me, first civil contact I have had with her and I am throbbing my love rod deep into her helm of unknown amusement. Sad and pathetic – should have jerked off before I came to pick her up.

It is amazing how wonderful these charity events can be, the money spent in order to get money to give away, the whole transaction leaves the receiver better off than they were before in terms of assistance but not as much as you would expect. It is grand this party, party for the poor, party for the needy, organized by the rich and enjoyed by the rich, a façade, a theatrical exhibition of how generous we rich folks are, that we take a precious day from our rigorous pursuit to earn more than we need to give less than infinitesimal fraction of it to those that need and deserve and merely enjoy ourselves while doing it. I give away in private more than this party will collect today, yet I am here to show that I can grace the poor with a few alms and be glorified for it.

Look at them smiling; look at them drinking heartiest from their flasks of pity, enjoying themselves. O' yes indeed I am donating 50,000 dollars to the aid of African children, of course you are, how kind of you to do such a deed. That 50,000 will buy the children new parents, a new memory to replace the graphic rape of their mothers in front of their innocent eyes and the slitting of their fathers' throats. And you, you are giving away 100,000 oh my oh my, that will help the poor kids to be fed for a generation and how gloriously they will feed while watching so many of the others die of hunger and become forever dependent on your pity. No amount of money can relinquish the misery it causes in attaining it, no one can escape this evil, no one. We all know how greed fuels the children of tomorrow to suffer, throwing few back at them will only ease our guilt nothing more; enjoy, dance, be merry and let those with a conscience writhe in guilt yet make plenty more in shameless delight.

"Are you all right? You look sick." Sick, of course I am sick, what else do you expect me to feel?

I look at her, she knows what I am feeling, I don't know how I know but I have a feeling that she knows, and for some reason I think she is feeling the same, but knows better not to indulge in such feelings. "My apologies, these looks are nothing but superficial. I shall move about and get some air, I am sure you wish to mingle free."

"Only if you are sure you are fine." She seems a bit disappointed, I know you are – your knight in shining armour is not so proud of his armour.

"I am, go I am sure there are a lot awaiting your company." I say it with as much reassurance as I can muster, my soul is shivering. How sickening this display seems? It has affected me always in the same manner but why does it do so strongly today? I need to hold it together, anger and sadness combined.

She looks at me a bit confused but more annoyed. "Most don't know that I am even here, coming here was your idea, getting to know me better. I understand you are reluctant for people to know we came here together."

Yes, you are right. What was I thinking? Although most people already know we are to be together, that is downright absurd thinking, but I did bring you here myself – getting to know you better, are you getting to know me better? "No it is not like that …"

"Please, don't insult me. I will let you be till you find your way back to me. Just don't forget you are my ride back, unless you wish for me to be lost among these greedy slimes." I am sure none have more greed than what slithers in my home.

"I .." Yes, not my finest hour.

"Later if not sooner." She goes away, not sad or even disappointed but just a bit annoyed. Again, annoyed. I thought I was the only one being annoyed with our exchanges of lately but I guess I was wrong. At least she understands something is wrong and is willing to let me sort it out myself. Although to be honest I do not really know what is wrong myself. So self-consuming.

I have always had a conscience, even though I have made money for these past years by hook or crook mostly as our company motto stands by crook. But this new found enforced uneasy conscience is a bit disturbing to my senses. People live and die every day, it is not my doing but it does seem to be my undoing. Why did Gilbert advise me of this? He knows I am not suited for charity events especially how the last one went. He knows I do not like going to one unless I am hosting myself, at least than I can invite people who I know are going to make a difference to others and not just themselves. Considering how the last one went, why did I ever agree to come here? The only good thing was seeing that girl in last event. Hmm ... something about her, so unnaturally alluring.

And there she is again. I do not believe it. It's her, yes. Galadriel is nowhere in sight, I should make my approach. But is it wise? half of the people here know I am to be engaged to her and married, is it wise? Have I ever done anything wise?

I should introduce myself to her. What if she knows who I am and just thinks of me a horny philanthropist? Well, I can introduce myself, doesn't mean I have to flirt with her. Why didn't I consider that option? How bad can it go? -

"Fancy meeting you here, again." I am really off my game today.

She turns around and looks at me, at me, at my overzealous booming smiling face. Why the hell am I smiling like a horny teenager? "Again? I don't think we ever met before this forceful intrusion."

Forceful? Not as if you were talking with anyone, just going through your phone. "I didn't get a chance to introduce myself last time, but I noticed you." Noticed you, really? Noticed you? Seriously?

O' cat eyes, mean eyes, she is going to kill me, "Noticed me? By that you mean you were staring at me like a horny kid and watching my every move. I wouldn't have mind you following me from one ass cheek to another if you at least had enough decency to donate something for the charity I was supporting the other night."

"Well I ..." Not going as planned.

"Just forget about it, can you please go bother someone else? I have got enough stories to dig up on these rich snobs than to worry about you as well." Now that I notice, well I have to notice something else since her ass is the other way around, she has hidden recorder. She had been recording in secret – there are so many stories to unravel over here. At least she isn't one of them. So interesting.

"So you are a journalist?" Not a good one though, if you cannot even pick out one of the youngest billionaires out of a basket full of the so called snobs.

She turns sideways, searching for someone, maybe her next victim out of so many, "Yes, Sherlock. So perceptive yet can't take a hint."

Better let her be on her way. "My apologies, I shall make myself scarce."

How bad can it go I said? Well not worse than this. "Sooner the better." She looks at me for a last time, she is trying to recognize me but she cannot. Sir Drexly walks by near us; she catches a last glimpse and goes off in pursuit. As she is going, Miss Maurice, a renowned daughter of the most ferociously enterprising industrialist waves towards me. She is the first to notice me here, blows a kiss towards me in her awkward joshing manner as always and shouts out, "Johann Blakemore as I live and breathe, Dad was looking for you, you trouble maker." The journalist looks towards me again, Johann, yes you recognize me now. A bit too late, she knows it; she looks away in embarrassment and continues towards Sir Drexly. I feel like I just walked in on a romantic novel cliché. Mistaken identity, dashing billionaire chasing after a career driven women, is turned down. I have a feeling we will meet again.

"Is it too soon?" Yes of course it is, it's hardly been ten minutes. Galadriel, okay perhaps I will start mentioning her as she prefers Gladys, rolls her hand smoothly around my waste.

"Not soon enough." Yes of course, now I know how to play it smooth.

"What happened?" Why would you assume something happened? But something did happen. I mean for one, I do not recognize most of the people over here. They all seem to be the nieces and nephews of someone important, apart from Maurice and Peter Drexly as far as I have noticed. What is going on? No one cares for Africa anymore, or should I say no one cares to be seen caring for Africa anymore? And secondly, I just got annihilated by a stunning girl. Did you see that? Of course you didn't, I am glad you didn't but you should have. "Nothing, nothing. Just a misunderstanding. Someone mistook me for a nobody." To sum it up.

"Can you blame them? You are the only one here not in a tux." Yes, well I didn't know it was going to be like this, did I?. And it's not my fault its Gilby's fault. He told me to wear this. "Well I didn't think ..."

She stops me mid-sentence, "Let's not think." Don't you start as well now! "Yes let's not. I don't feel like being here any longer. Would you mind if we just went home?" I say in the most, I don't want to go to school today, way as possible.

"Only if you promise to take me to dinner tomorrow." Why are you so nice to me? It is disturbing yet comforting. "I would like nothing better." One of these days my pants are really going to explode.

She looks at me, searching for something in me with the saddest of faces yet bearing the warmest of smiles and says, "These sudden changes in your mood towards me are sometimes very unsettling." They are to me as well; you and the journalist both are starting to become more complex than I wanted it to be.

It is amazing how much comfort you can find in a glass of a fine scotch, and much more in a whole bottle yet such comfort eludes me. After all that has gone through my head today, I cannot find my thoughts wondering further away from that of my father. What is that old bastard hiding? What was in that letter? My suspicions about his past are taking shape and making me rethink a lot of things.

"Johann, what on Earth is the matter with you?" What the what, who the … "What?" Exactly, what? Where did he come from? He should be in bed?

"Have you just got home or have you been sitting here since last night?" Gilby says with the slightest bit of concern in his tone, seems to be taken aback by that 'what', but I can assure you that 'what' was not misplaced. Why is everyone bent on breaking my chain of thoughts?

"Everyone was wearing a tux you know?" I might as well tell him that, I mean everyone was in their best attire with the bow tie and what have you not, and there I was in a leisure suit.

He looks at me with a vacant surprised face. You are surprised? Imagine the look on my face when I walked in that horrendous nightmare, I never looked so out of place in my entire life. "Well I am sorry, I thought you would skip the whole charity idea and go to dinner with Galadriel. Didn't want you to look like a fool in the restaurant. I even booked a table at the Lacroix. I left a note in your coat." Really? Are we playing treasure hunt now? "Why was it so hard to just say what you meant for me to do?" I cannot even be bothered with it, I just want to have a quiet drink with my thoughts, leave me alone you old fool.

"Is this what it's all about? I am so sorry. I am sure no one pointed out your fashion sense. That is no reason to sit here drinking all night, by yourself." All night? What? Yes again not misplaced, what the what the what. "What do you mean, all night? What time is it anyway?" I only went for a little stroll after I dropped her off and then came straight back to have a drink, well I had more than one but I am sure I didn't have that many. "It is 6'o clock in the morning." Well I suppose I had a bit too many then. 6, really 6?

"Oh my, I have been sitting here all night." To be honest I still don't really care, I still would like to be left alone. "What's wrong?" What is wrong? My father is forcing me to marry Gladys, and she is wonderful and delightful but still it seems a bit too pushy for my liking. I seem to like her but apparently I love being insulted and shouted at, some perplexing fetish of mine by Freudian analogy probably some repressed childhood indignation. Not to mention, over the past few months I have found some disconcerting discrepancies in our company's accounts which are dated back to its establishment. I am not for absolute business ethics but they seem more shady than usual with the alarm bells of my dad has been a rotten goblin for longer than I have known him. And yes, there is that matter with that letter, what was in that bloody letter. And speaking of letters the CIA is trying to get it touch with me – the fucking CIA. They believe my father has become a traitor to the nation. "It's nothing. I never knew being insulted could seem so arousing to me." Did I say that out loud? "What are you on about?" Guess I did.

"Oh never mind. I need to go to the city tomorrow morning, got a meeting early after with the board of directors. Can you please make the arrangements?" No my Gliby I am not telling you a single thing unless you tell me first what is eating you. "Yes, ofcourse."

"And if you don't mind can I have my breakfast a bit early? I don't really feel like going to sleep now." Perhaps I will open the fifth black envelope and have a little read.

"What would you like?"

"Anything that goes well with scotch."

---

"You are up early for once." The cold harsh pulsating vocals from the crevasses of hell, so early in the morning yet so late in the depths of my sinking night. "Aren't you the ardent observer?" He is staring at me, with disdain and a hint of association; I care not to return the favour. I can feel him easing his stare, trying to settle back into his snide ways, "I heard you took Gladys to some charity event yesterday. Good to finally see you coming to your senses. I would say 'back to' but you never had any to begin with." I still care not father of what you think, and I care not to play your game. It has grown grey on my frown. "I can assure you I have more sense to notice your conniving business acumen."

"She is not just a business acquisition. She is to be your brain surgeon. I am done having you run around like a monkey tarnishing my reputation." Reputation? That is the one and truly only thing we both have in common, reputation lurks not in our midst. Why is he trying to provoke me? "Monkey? I will have you know this monkey has made more money for your crooked company in the past five years than you have over your lifetime." And why am I getting provoked?

"Yes, and I want to make sure you keep on doing that for the many more to come." He picks up my whiskey bottle and pours himself a glass. So you think not being a part of your past or present will somehow make me want to be a part of your future. "Oh, I don't know why I even bother talking with you." Maybe I wanted to say something more significant, but I cannot be bothered to do that as well and why must I?

We sit in silence, thinking how best to suppress the thoughts. We drink and we drink, drown our conversations in drunken trepidations. How much we hate each other's existence, can such emotions ever be measured? Why do I even bother coming to this suffocating cave of such a heartless monster, why do I still call this home? I know there is no hope, no hope to ever establish any decent relationship between the two of us. Is this what he is trying to do with this marriage? Is this why he is forcing this upon me? So we have some sort of common ground? The more I try to think about it the more it shakes my mind in an endless stream of screaming misery. Why is it so hard for me to say no to him? What is this fear that draws me towards him and wants me to run as far away as I can? I will marry her, but I will not be a part of his scheme or let her fall unto his curse.

"Don't think for a second that my agreement to this communion has anything to do with my fondness towards you." I say while trying to hold myself as much as I can to not say it.

"There has never been any fondness between us, no reason for me to establish such thoughts so well into my comfortable years. But I am glad nonetheless to hear you agree." I can feel his teeth grinding as well.

I get up and leave the room; I do not want to look into his eyes at this moment of solitary agreement in our lives. Today is not about me and not about him and definitely not about us. Today is about me coming to terms with the path I must now take. Oh well in some way it is about me, and well the path I am choosing is taking up the CIA on their offer and digging up his past so it is about him as well, and me, him make an us so it is about us as well – I guess I am slightly more drunk than I thought I was, let's go eat my breakfast.

It seems so silent here, no wind playing tag with the leaves today, the whole forest is asleep or just sharing my grief. There is not a single day that goes by that I don't miss you mother, I just wish I had enough time to know you better. So many things I could talk to you about, things that I am left alone to just ponder with myself. As always I sit beside her grave, and talk to her with long pauses of nothingness as I try my best to remember her.

"Everything is ready; let me know when you want us to leave," ever the sentimental my dear Gilby. "I am starting to forget her face little by little, all I can remember is her smell on a warm summer's day and the smell of garlic sizzling in butter, she always used to put so much garlic. Is it sad that all I can remember is her cooking me lunch?" I gaze at her grave like always just expecting her to reach out of it so we can just pick up where we left off. "I like garlic. And no it is not sad Johann, you knew your mother and you loved her and she loved you, and you know that. Some of us don't even get to experience that wonderful feeling of unconditional love." I look at him and I can see real sadness in his eyes, he does try his best to hide it, "I love you unconditionally Gilbert." A smirk from me and a smirk from him, mine more of content in knowing I have annoyed him to an uncomfortable level, his more of an acknowledgement of we better leave this conversation for another time. "No point being serious around you is there, come on now, you have been here for at least 3 hours. We have to get going to make it back in good time. Off to the big city." He has turned back to his close shell, good, I need him like that for now. "I am not going to Manhattan, I am off to London. The flight is already booked, it leaves in the morning. I am going to stay in a hotel overnight." I forgot to tell him that, come to think of it, would have been a lot easier if I let him arrange everything for me, he can be more discreet than me in these matters. "All right, well why not take the private jet, we will be in time for tea or a pint of the most ugly if you prefer."

Discreet Gilbert, I need to be discreet. What part of discreet don't you understand, seriously? I shall revise my judgement from a second ago and instead commend myself for making all the arrangements on my own. "No I wish to go there unnoticed, and I am going on my own, I have few things to take care of." The wind is back, cold wind on a warm day is the most soothing sensation ever known. Feels like yesterday, when we used to take long walks in this forest, me and my dearly departed mother. I always used to stop to feel the wind, a gush of cold wind, prickling my senses, telling me the secrets of the old. How I wish for that kid to be born again?! I look towards Gilbert, who seems to have gone a bit silent, does he finally understand the gravity of the situation, I wonder? All is not well in our world and it hasn't been for a very long time. But I cannot take it anymore; the only way I can move on is by knowing that I can move on. "There is something I need to find out Gilby, something is not right. That is why I want you to be here, my father is up to something and we need to figure out what."

"What good will it bring?" He is not looking at me, he is starring at my mother's grave. Such deep sadness in his voice, yet a submissive aggression entwined with a desire to be led to destruction rather than lead away from it. He knows something I don't, apart from a billion other things, he knows something about what burns me more than what he lets on. But interrogating him will not lead me anywhere, all shall be revealed in good time.

"A lot, even if for my peace of mind. I have been looking a lot into the company finances and there are a lot of discrepancies. I need to figure out what are the actual foundations of this company." I know there is something connected with my father, his immense fortunes, my mother's sudden death, this girl I am supposed to marry and possibly Gilbert as well, and according to CIA – the Nazis, hail the fat evil dick, but I just cannot connect the dots, not yet.

He looks towards me finally with his ever so bright soul searching eyes and says, "If you don't agree with what he does, you can always just leave this all. You have enough money to start your own business or do whatever you want. Sometimes I do not understand your reluctance to give yourself the pleasure of a normal life. You don't have to live under his rule just leave it and go." With his hand on my shoulder he couldn't have sounded less convincing of his earnest even if he tried. I know, he cares for me deeply, and I know he wants me to get away from all this and begin anew where happiness might blossom without any fear of decay. But I know as well that he wants me to find the truth, more than he knows so that he can be at peace knowing what he doesn't, yet.

"No. I will destroy him from inside out. I do not ignore things, Gilbert. I will know what he is up to and I will destroy him, every last bit of him. I want him to see it happening, I will not rest until I have my ultimate revenge. And no do not even think about it Gilbert, try to understand, I don't want to kill him I want to destroy him to a point where he wants to kill himself." I am shaking with anger, with tears contemplating whether to form a river or a dam. Stuck, subdued emotions, regressive memories, throat all choked up, all I can see is red but I know it will pass in a second. I don't want it to pass, why do I stop myself from my own desired expressions? I want to burst, I want to let it all out but I cannot. He holds my face in his big comforting hands and looks at me, taking a deep breath, looks at me. "I understand, I just don't think your mother would like you to harbour that much hatred for anyone. Anyway what do you want me to do then?" I am sure she wouldn't have wanted to die unexpected as well; life doesn't always work out as we imagine. "You are to stay over here my friend, and find out as much as you can by whatever means necessary." Goodbye mother, don't worry I will make him pay for what he did to you, I promise.

Why am I going to London? Yes, I had a feeling you might be wondering about that. The last letter in a black envelope that I received from the CIA I actually opened it. It told me that I should visit old alliances to start my journey of discovery. Also told me to get an overnight stay at a specific motel where my CIA coordinator or handler will liaise with me regarding best tactics to proceed. So this will be my first meet with them, officially, although my suspicions do not need validation from them. The early finances of the company are a bit dodgy to say the least and the timing of the inception of our company is no mere coincidence as well. I know my father was in Germany during World War II, there are no records of which side he fought or even if he fought or not. His family was substantially rich but not as much as it got straight after the end of WWII. His parents, my grandparents had already died a long time ago, with sizeable inheritance to be shared by three brothers, but obviously only he survived the war and came back to fortune. Now him having money from his parents and starting the whole company is a cover up as far as I can see, because the inheritance was nowhere enough to explain it although it has been made to seem that way. If CIA has fears that my father is a traitor that can only mean that he was with the Nazi Regime, made money robbing and stealing innocents and came back when all started falling down. He must have been a trader in those times, buying stuff on cheap from scared Jews trying to run away and then selling for a profit, or he could be one of main players in Her Hitler's circle. It's all conjecture at this time but I just know in my guts that if it's during the Second World War he made money; he had to be in some way on the wrong side. But why is the CIA looking into it now, after all these years, and why ask me to help them look into it. Surely if his past is that well-hidden it must have been done by CIA themselves – I need to connect the dots.

I haven't stayed in such small motels for a very long time, well I have never stayed in a motel but for some reason I feel like I did. It is, let's say doable. It is not as tragic as many would make it out to be. I guess the only problem is the other shady characters that I can sense occupying other rooms. Apart from that it got all the basic necessities, although at the ultimate basic level but it is still there. I might seem spoiled but to be honest I have never felt as such. Yes, I enjoy the luxuries afforded towards me but who wouldn't? Doesn't mean that I cannot live without them. Every time I went to Europe to disappear for few months at a time, I always lived in basic accommodations. I don't know why, but it somehow puts everything into perspective, there are better things in life to spend your time and money on than yourself.

It is a good thing Gilbert forced me to eat something before I left, I am not being picky but I am not a fan of overly fatted up food, which seems to be the only sustenance around for miles. Coming here by taxi was a brilliant idea as well; I am filled with bright ideas today. I know, why am I staying over here? It is not like my father cannot find out where I am if he wanted to, I know that is what you are thinking. There is another reason; I am meeting the CIA agent here, remember? Someone you would not expect to meet in nice places, actually I am wrong – you cannot have any expectations of them from my experience so far you can expect anything and nothing of them. But I need to find evidence to such a claim, a Nazi enriched past and I still don't want it to be true even though I hate him till my last drop. I cannot believe how many of them managed to escape with or without aid, escape without even a hint of lawsuit looming on top of them. It doesn't matter if they were not fully committed to Hitler's cause, they were still part of the organization, making up the numbers, making the regime strong that took the lives of so many and uprooted generations into the mind numbing reality of human cruelty, still they walk free. If not hanged they should have been locked up for good, I know I am contradicting my own existence by saying that, but it would be just.

'Knock, knock', ah that must be him. I am so wound up right now I just might end up slitting his throat than taking his help uncovering the mysteries of my Nazi father. Woo where did that come from, I guess my subconscious finds similarities between Nazis' and CIA, must be some reason for that association, maybe my mind knows something I don't. My face is red with fury, my body shaking with disgust as I open the door, ready to put one between his eyes. Maybe I just don't like black envelopes, but we both know its not true – its the best colour for an envelope. I believe I forgot to mention I was carrying a gun. I am as of nature completely against guns and the violence they entertain in their love affair. But I cannot go on a dangerous fact finding route without equipping myself with the necessary defensive tools. It is self-contradictory – two contradictions in a single page - how one thing; one main proprietary act induced by guns that I am against is what I find myself completely committed to doing.

"Now is that the best way to greet your bride to be." I am in shock, the hatred brooded up is still there but the projection cannot be implemented. I am still starring at her, point blank like an idiot. "Can you please put that down now? You are making me nervous." I am still holding the gun in her face, she does look nervous now. I throw my gun down and grab hold of her and kiss her as I have never kissed another before. She resists but then gives in; she knows what is going on. This is no time to hold back, it is time to let go and to let the passion flow. Still in the lock of intense lust I pick her up and throw her on the bed, her sensual touch to my skin has already made my senses wild. There is an aura of love lost in lust looming above us, for once I wish to forget my existence and just express myself physically. And that we do, and so I stop thinking, the time for thinking has been taken over by the time for feeling. Her skin is milky softness, nurtured for so carefully, her lips like melted raspberries straight from heaven onto mine. All of a sudden she grabs hold of me, throws me on my back and jumps on top of me. "Let me show you what sex is all about." That's the last thing I remember till I wake up from the blissful waking dream after well over an hour. I look over at her, now calm and satisfied, the transformation is astonishing and I wish to see it over and over again.

"Are you not going to ask me why I am here?" She says without looking at me, maybe aware of me observing her beautiful personality spread out butt-naked on my side. "We can leave that till morning." I say to her while pulling her closer to me and kissing her neck. "I thought your flight was tonight." She knows about my flight, she comes with more motive than I know. And where is that CIA agent. But that can still wait till the morning. "My flight is in the morning, why don't you show me how much more damage you can do to my back." She turns towards me and gives me a kiss, which said no more. "I have to leave soon I cannot stay for long."

Well that is disappointing, but perhaps for the best. What was I thinking? That guy still might show up at some point in the night, I cannot have her over here for that. She shouldn't know what I intend to do in London. Wait, how does she know about my flight and about me staying here?

"Do you know where I am going?" I look at her trying to catch something out but to no avail.

"Yes I know, you are going to London. Gilbert told me. And he also told me you will be staying here. So don't worry I am not spying on you. To be honest Gilbert dropped me off over here, and he will be here soon to pick me up." She starts gathering her stuff and starts putting her clothes back on.

I was supposed to go off in secret, this is absolutely ridiculous. I do not understand why Gilbert trusts her so much. Her father has been the longest known associate of my father, which cannot be good. "I didn't mean it like that.

It was just supposed to be a secret escape and obviously I didn't want anyone to know about it. I have some business to take care of in London and I didn't want anyone else involved with it."

"Don't worry sweet Johann; your secret is safe with me. You were supposed to take me for dinner, remember. It's all right; it's not as if I don't have others to take me out for dinner. I just wanted to see you before you went, and make sure you are not trying to run away from me." Can it be just that innocent? I doubt it but I will go with it for now.

"I am not trying to run away from you, I just want to take care of few things and a bit of space from you know who for a little while." She pears through the blinds and spots someone in the parking lot. She comes over and gives me a kiss. "Safe travels Johann and thank you for the dinner." She smiles, which makes me smile, and opens the door. "O' I almost forgot Johann, someone came over your house, a guy in a very government standard suit, you know what I mean. Left this letter for you, told him to call you, but he said you prefer letters, that is actually what I came to give you before you went crazy." A black envelope, I take it from her and throw it on the bed just to pretend it's important for me to take it but not important enough for me to open it straight away. She smiles once again looking deeply in my eyes, and goes off.

I wait for hours and that agent never show up. Her coming over here, while him going missing doesn't seem that much of a coincidence to me. I do not have any way to contact him; I guess I will just have to find another way of knowing what I need to know. Wait, the envelope, I still haven't opened it, how long have I been just staring at the ceiling. I been laying on it all this time, what is wrong with me? I take the envelope from underneath me and open it. And, I don't prefer letters, why would that agent say that? Come to think of it, why was she at my house?

*'Johann, there wasn't enough time to meet you, to be honest I had better things to do than meet you. Everyone will know that you have gone to London, you should have just openly gone, there was no reason to make it so difficult for yourself. Either way you have to make up some excuse, a reason to be there, I suggest an independent investment you need to make separate from company perhaps an acquisition of some sort, I don't know just make something up – but be aware that whatever you make up you actually have to do it to make it believable.*

*Anyway, there is a guy in London, Alexander. He has the information that we need, but for some reason – well a very good reason – that slime will not meet us in person. Arrange a meeting with him, midnight - Friday, hear what he has to say, buy what he has to sell, do whatever you have to just make sure you squeeze every inch of information out of him. Safe flight.'*

Not that dramatic like the other letters from CIA, and to be honest not much of a letter, just a note, rudely written and really risky to be writing letters with plans or partial plans either way vital information. Anyway at least I know the dickhead isn't coming, I can go to sleep.

I put my leather suitcase down after opening the door of my apartment. It is still the same, not even an inch is different from how I left it. I have to say Colin really does look after this place well. And just as I was thinking such thoughts I sense someone behind me. I would be shocked beyond all recognition if that turns out to be Galadriel again. But as I turn around to my dismay it is only Colin, Mr Colin Smith.

"Good evening sir, why did you not tell me sooner that you were coming I would have cleaned it all up, and perhaps put something in the oven to nourish your appetite? They provide horrible food on the planes, you must be starving." They do not really give that much horrible food on the planes, well at least not in first class. But there is no point mentioning all of that to poor old Colin. I should mention I am in London now, I thought I would spare you the plane journey and to the apartment. Well I say it's an apartment, it's more like a mansion on stilts. I do like London better than New York, but it's for personal reasons more than anything.

"Colin, my dear friend, the place looks perfect you have no need to worry. But I wouldn't mind something out of the oven. I am actually starving."

"Don't you mind that sir, as soon as I got to know you were coming around, I had my partner cook something for you, I brought it with me, and I will just heat it up and get it ready for you. You go on freshen up and leave the rest to me." He takes my coat and my suitcase, and gives me a warm look, the kind of look that only comes from genuine care.

"So you did get something for me to eat, what are you worried about then?"

"Well, if we had known it earlier then Brian would have made something special for you."

"Oh yes that's right Brian, your Brian. How is he? I have not seen him for ages. The Head Chef at Langham."

"So kind of you to remember, and very apt of you to know that he is Head Chef now – last time you guys met he was a Sous Chef. Anyway, he is doing quite well."

"I hope you got enough for two, because I am not going to have my dinner alone."

"Of course, don't be silly, I won't let you have it alone, this stuff is too good not to share."

"How have you both been, Colin?"

"We are getting on fine, don't you worry about us. Times are hard, certain people still haven't grown to accept us. We still have to persevere, but we will be fine as long as we have each other. Now, look you have made me all emotional. Go on, freshen up." I go off to my room and straight into the shower. When I am in the states all I want to do is go out and about, do something, be productive. But when I come here, I just feel like I want to cosy up in front of a fire cuddled in a warm blanket.

I come back out to find Colin waiting for me at the table. I sit myself down, and without much ceremony start eating straight away.

"This is absolutely delicious, Colin. You are so lucky to have him." Perfectly cooked duck, so tender, and this gravy sauce whatever it is made of, is so well balanced. I am no expert in these matters, but I know good food when I eat it.

"I guess I am." He says without much enthusiasm, there is something wrong with him. What is up with these brothers, hiding something from me all the bloody time? Another thing I forgot to mention Colin is Gilbert's brother. I do not think that anyone apart from me knows that Colin is Gilbert's brother, which is why they have different surnames. I do not exactly know why it is such a secret, but I made a promise long ago – and when it comes to Gilbert I do not tend to ask many questions.

"Now come on, why the long face? What is bothering you?" I cannot really take much of my attention away from this delicious duck, as much as I care for Colin, this is just too damn good. I feel as if I have not been fed for days. I am not really sure what is it about Brain's cooking, every time I eat it, I feel as if I have been lost and found a million times.

He looks at me, wanting to say something but not at the same time. He drops his head a little and I know he is going to deflect the actual thought to a more obscure one. "Oh it's nothing sir, it is just so depressing sometimes to see the world filled with so much hatred. Why are people more concerned about other people's doings than their own? We are less than a decade away from new millennia still some people tend to live in the dark ages."

Sometimes there is just no winning with these two brothers, why do they feel the need to hide their actual emotions to me. "It is the way we are, but certainly not the way we ought to be. I guess we are all scared, and anything different just puts us completely off."

"How is Gilbert?" Ah some real emotions at last, I was waiting for him to ask me that.

"Your brother is doing just fine, getting older and more secretive than you. You should talk to him." His eyes meet mine for a second and then they wander off, as if agreeing but knowing not much can be done about it. "Anyway, you still haven't told me why you have come all the way over to London." He says lazily while still not looking at me, deflection – they are both consistent with their annoyance.

I might as well not probe, there is no point. Whatever is going on between them I do not feel it is my place to repair it. "I came to see you of course."

He looks at me now, with a smile, almost a wounded smile, "That is very kind of you but we both know that is not true. I heard your father wanted to close down all business here."

"He already has Colin; all the businesses in Europe have been sold over the last two year."

"But how come no one got to know about it? And why, were they not profitable enough?" It confuses me as well.

"No they were quite profitable as far as I know, I am not sure why they have been sold, I was never given full details on all European businesses of my father you know and to be honest I was never interested enough to ask. The reason why no one got to know about it, is because all of them are still working under their own name, only the parent company has switched hands, plus the deals are just about being finalized. Soon there will a major press conference about it and what not."

"It is very strange, why would your father sell all businesses in Europe, not just from here but elsewhere as well?" Really? I do not think so it is that strange, I think so it's perfectly normal for someone trying to hide something.

"And it is precisely because of this reason why I have come here." It is true in some way.

"Well I do not blame you for searching the truth but you have to protect yourself. Now we both know that carrying arms is not as common over here as it would be back home. But you do need to have some." He knows more than what I think, something or someone – more perhaps someone – scares him. "I do not think it would be necessary Colin."

"If we are both on the same page, than I know what dangerous waters you might be testing. In that case you do need some protection." No we are not on the same page; to be honest we are not even on the same book. "Don't worry, it is taken care of."

"That's good to know." He gives me a concerned look, a very genuine one. "No harm in being cautious, now would you like a glass of whiskey and a cigar to relax?"

Finally, something to dull my senses, "That would be nice."

"I will set up the fireplace, go on I will clear up the plates afterwards." He gives me a bit of an affectionate nudge.

"Thank you, but Colin I do not want you to wait on me all the time I am over here."

"It is no trouble; you are my employer after all." Employer, it is such a cold word. I guess it is only fair, I am expecting him to tell me something he knows while I do not feel I need to tell him what I know.

"Yes but I do not want you to feel that way. You are closer than family to me."

"In that case I will bring two glasses of whiskey if you don't mind."

He has taken care of me more than anyone else when I was only a kid, and my father didn't want to do anything with me. Him and Gilbert, have always been there for me. I do not know for what reason only I know that he is Gilbert's brother, why is it such a big secret.

"You do that; I will set up the fireplace." I was sent to school in London, it was nice to have someone here who really cared about me like I was their own.

---

There is a feeling of disconnection with the rest of the world that I have become accustomed to overtime. But I cannot still feel completely out of this world, inferior or superior. I still find myself caring for it and the inhabitants of it. How strange a feeling is that to experience yet we know it to be true because there are others out there that feel the same. The world and the living organisms in it are of a physical nature and an ideological nature as well. You hate an idea, feel disconnected towards it or are completely ignorant towards it while it is there, present for someone else to admire and accept it. In the same world with the same things it creates different existences of it. So I say I feel disconnected with this world and at the same time I don't – because it not the world I feel disconnected with but the idea of it that we have created. Just an insane thought from an insane mind grown bored of its own existence I presume.

As soon as I step outside the building after a million pointless questions asked by me and a billion asked of me, I get swarmed by journalists, time for them to ask me some pointless questions.

'Why do you think all your American friends are suddenly interested in buying our clubs?'

'How do you find the weather?'

'What are you trying to achieve with this acquisition?'

'Can your investment finally bring the club to premier league?'

'Did you ever play football when you were young?'

'Why Leyton Orient?'

I really need to calm this situation down. I cannot elbow my way through this, although I am more inclined to head-butt my way through them. Oh I forgot to mention, I have put a bid in to buy Leyton Orient, it is a soccer or rather football club in case you didn't know. I had to make it as a personal investment and I think I want to invest in sports. I could have gone for more secure investment and bought a Hotel or a chain of them but there is no fun in there. Actually I have already done that as well, that's how Brian was made Head Chef all of a sudden and will be made General Manager in a few months' time should he wish to be one. I have always liked soccer, I made few enquiries before coming over and here I am now. Buy a club here, then maybe one back home and another somewhere else in Europe, Germany might be appropriate given my heritage. Come to think of it as soon as I made enquiries regarding the sale of the club and my intentions to take over given that FA approves it everyone knew I would be coming over to England. I mean no one knew when but they knew I would be coming to make it official. Why did I bother with the whole secret escape? What was the point of that? Should have just got my private jet in and be more comfortable. It was an incredibly stupid thing to do, but anyway it is done, I think I just get caught up sometimes in the excitement of the situation. I need to put these thoughts away; it is time to concentrate on dealing with these jackals right now.

"All right just settle down, let me see. It's damp and cold but it doesn't bother me. Investments are investments no matter where and in what they are, but I haven't made any yet. I am trying to achieve what everyone does, success. And what was that last one, yes why Leyton Orient? Well, why not? Now if you would excuse me, I have to get back to my life."

Just as I finish smirking and start weaving my way past them with a lot of other questions being thrown at me, I notice someone in the midst of all the faces, the charity journalist. We share a moment and then our eyes get torn apart trying to remember but it seems she can't really remember. I didn't know she covered sports journalism as well and that also in England; come to think of it her accent was very English but I didn't make much of it before. She didn't even ask any questions or did she? I go back to my car and drive away, confused and dazed. Maybe she just covers rich guys making unnecessary headlines – she must have an angle.

Stuck in traffic, obvious conclusion to a mistake well made. Absolutely useless driving a car in London. Come to think of it, I do not remember driving a car to the meeting. As a matter of fact my car is still in my garage, I hired a car and a driver to go the meeting. A driver who left the keys in the car and probably now wondering where the car has gone. I guess I am not much in the habit of being driven around. Let's give him a call,

"Ah hello, Mr Driver", do not really know his name, "Where are you?"

"I am in the boot, been banging for the past 10 minutes." He seems scared and agitated, and slightly angry. I wonder why he is stuck in the trunk of his own car.

"Why didn't you just call me?"

"I am sorry sir, but my hands were tied up, only managed to get them off. And I had been calling, but you were listening to music so loud."

I check my phone, and there had been quite a few missed calls, "But Mr. driver what are doing in the boot?"

"I can tell you all if you would be kind enough to get me out of here please." He seems a bit annoyed now; don't blame him, "Of course!"

I drive into one of the side roads, there is too much traffic anyway might as well take the guy out of the trunk. I find a bit of quite place, park the car and to everyone's amazement I open the trunk and out came a guy. Well everyone's amazement is a bit of an exaggeration; there are only four people over here, if you want to count the cat that seems to have got the hiccups. It's one of the back alleys and the other three seemingly humans do not really pay much attention to it. I guess these types of things might happen here often.

'Ok Sir, we have to leave this car here and report it to the police." He says while taking his phone out and dialling the emergency services. I take the phone from his hand, smash it on the floor and kick it to oblivion. "We will do no such thing, you will call your company and tell them I hated the car so much that I made you drive to the scrapyard and got it dismantled and destroyed. I will pay in full for the car and loss of business."

"But sir …."

"Don't worry; just tell me who did what and why."

"You didn't really have to smash my phone; it wasn't the company phone it was mine." Well, yes I didn't really have to do that, I do not know why I did it.

"Tell you what, here is thousand pounds, I had planned to give it to someone who needed it today and it seems to me that you need it. Go on, take it, you can buy a better phone." I had a thousand pound in cash with me, might as well, poor guy needs it. It does seem an excessive amount to carry in cash right? Maybe for you but not for me, for me its lose change. And I actually have a lot more than that on me. I was really planning to give it to a homeless person who I saw earlier yesterday not too far off my apartment. I guess he can have it some other day.

"Now can you please tell me …."

And so he told me everything, a bit too much. I am not going to bore you with all the unnecessary details. Basically two guys put him in the trunk of the car, one of them pretended to be the driver and the other my bodyguard. They were waiting for me to come back. Well since he was at this point in the trunk so he is not entirely sure what had happened but they got spooked and ran off, leaving him all tied up still in the trunk and the keys in the car. Interesting, but I am not sure if it is interesting enough. I feel hungry; hope there is a decent eatery around here.

"Okay thank you for all that, I am going to go off now, Good luck with the rest of your life Mr Driver." He nods and makes a move towards the car. "Mr Driver, what are you doing?"

"I am taking it to the scrapyard sir, like you wanted."

"No, you are going back to your company or home or wherever you want. You are leaving the car where it is. Look here is another £500 and by the time you get back, a representative of mine will be there to pay the car off. Don't worry you won't get it trouble."

"As you wish."

"Are you ready to order, sir?"

"Yes I am, can I have a pork pie with green olives and glaze of honey?"

"I will get him for you sir, may I know what is it regarding?"

"I didn't get enough cheese in my salad."

"Sorry to hear that sir, he won't be long."

"Good get me two glasses of your finest scotch while I wait."

"Very well, sir."

Bizarre I know, but when you are in my position which most of you would not be, you can never be too careful. I have my people in places most unexpected, money can make your worst enemy loyal like a sick puppy.

"Your drinks sir, he is making you something special himself."

"Good, I haven't been sick in a while, looking forward to it."

Slow country music is playing in the restaurant, doesn't match the ambience at all but Bill is crazy about country. Everyone has their vice I guess, I am not sure if I should call it that. It's what makes us who we are, something strange to go with the ordinary, or in his case something normal to go with his strange. Who am I to complain? A well accomplished multi-whatevernaire headbangs like a lunatic whenever given the opportunity.

"You will get more than sick if you keep eating my food Johann, my dearest friend." A man build like an ox with a gravel voice to go with it walks on from behind and sits himself next to me. He gives me a curious look while fondling with his well-kept beard, I don't remember him being so fat, I guess he has been eating more than cooking, "Have your drink chef."

He lets go of his beard, takes the glass revealing a hint of his numerous tattoos on his arms, and downs it in one go. A few drops dribble on his beard, but he seems least bothered, what are a few drops in the rain forest, "Someone tried to pull one on you?"

"Yes something funny, one giggled but his laughter has been scrapped." I have never liked the idea of downing drinks; I guess that's why I am not much fond of vodka. You need time to savour the taste otherwise there is no point to the whole concept of drinking.

He cracks a smile and waves to the waiter in the corner looking at us intently; he comes over in a shot. Bill whispers something in his ear, the waiter nods and shoots off signalling something to another waiter in the other corner. The first waiter than goes over to the door and changes the sign to closed, and locks the door. There weren't any customers in anyway; I guess I just came in before the lunch hour. The second waiter brings a bottle and tops up our glasses and goes away into the back, "so where did this all happen?"

"Does it matter?" He sits back and his hands on his enormous stomach, "It will when we have to go and clean up that mess, but I guess it doesn't right now."

He takes a sip this time, shakes his glass a bit and takes a long hard look at the ceiling as if trying to summon the Gods. I take a bite from the risotto he made, perfect as usual. Well not entirely perfect but even better, a taste I am familiar with. I let him ponder over as I ponder over the past.

See Bill used to be a nobody, actually more than a nobody among the common society, but an emerging somebody in the underbellies of the stench hole when I met him. I actually met him while he was doing time in prison, back when I used to live in London. I was only a scrawny student and he was a colossal of a man. For all his looks, he had a kind humble heart. Colin told me Bill, a friend of Brian's as it were to be, convicted for the wrong crime just because he looked like a criminal. Apparently an amazing chef, so one thing led to another and here he is now with a restaurant gifted from me to him along with the most cunning lawyers who got him out of that scrap. Even then I knew investment in such a person would prove to be most beneficial. He was never a criminal, but doesn't mean he has no connections; he has very useful ones, and a way to clean up the mess like nobody else.

"Are you okay to go home from here, or do you want one of my guys to drop you?" I guess he knows there are things that I need to get done. We have never been in an overly conversational relationship, although he did teach me how to cut onions without crying – I never learned.

"Here," I give him a note with address, "This is where I left the car, you know what to do with it, take the keys as well. One of your guys usually goes at this time to get few supplies, I will go with him in the van, and he can drop me off on his way." Bill doesn't like getting food supply deliveries from companies, he usually sends someone to get fresh supplies where they can actually see what they are getting.

"Are you sure?"

"Yes, just tell him to keep it silent, I have got a headache and I am in no mood of unnecessary chit-chat."

There are two hefty men outside my apartment building. They seem oblivious to everything and are just staring into the distance, with ear pieces, security, for whom I wonder.

I soon find out as I notice two more in front of my door, I walk towards them, they open the door for me and let me in. I am a bit too tired to complain, and they don't seem the CIA sort, so I am probably safe to go in for now. I find Colin chatting with one of them, a stoic built battle worn person. He is the homeless guy I was planning on giving some money to, just two blocks away from this place, sneaky sneaky. He has got few scars on his ever so tanned white face, come to think of it most of them have tanned faces; they can't be from this part of the world then. They must have recently come over.

"Now, now, Colin you are a married man, remember that." I say as I approach them, letting them know of my presence and also that I am not intimidated by all this. Colin blushes a little and makes his way towards the kitchen with a promise of tea and coffee for all. I turn my attention towards the man who was talking with Colin; he seems to be their leader whatever this group of people seem to be. "And you are?"

He stands up; he is more impressively built than I thought he was, "Berenger O' Brien, sir, your personal security escort." He is still standing, probably wants me to give my approval, "And who sent you?"

"I am assigned by your company with the express view of protecting you." His accent is South African if I am not mistaken. The four other men I saw, there was something strange about them. All were similar yet very different from each other. Mercenaries, my father sent hired mercenaries, this really doesn't make sense.

"My father sent you here."

"Sir, it is a company directive." He says avoiding the 'no not your father, the company sent me'. The board of directors have never taken such steps before; they have never intervened in my doings before like this. It cannot be them, and why would they assume I need protection. My father must be going very loopy for them to have lost all hope in him and decide to protect my interests instead.

"Sir ....."

"Oh shut up, do what you have to do, although I don't need any protection."

He looks at me a bit hurt by that sudden rudeness, I guess he wasn't expecting me to be an asshole, what else do you expect, he tries his best not to show his displeasure at my interruption,

"As I was about to say sir, we will respect your personal space but we will be escorting you everywhere for your protection."

"Very well, for now please escort your behind out of my lodging."

"Ofcourse, sir."

I knew someone was going to find out sooner or later, it might have been that old git who knows, keeping an eye on me making sure I don't fuck up his plans, whatever they might be. And what a cover story it was, me buying a soccer club, how would it have stayed quite, impossible. Everyone would have known, with most expressing concerns at me not buying within states first, or having no sporting knowledge. But now that I have had time to think about it, not the worst of ideas actually. I have more than enough in my personal reserve, to buy over and run a club completely independent of my company. With the acquisition of that Hotel as well, and two more to follow, I can build my own empire and let my father's burn to high heaven. Again I forgot, this personal diary business is a bit new to me. The point is noting down everything but I keep on forgetting to mention details that might not be overly important. You know how I mentioned earlier it wouldn't be exciting just buying a Hotel or a chain of Hotels, and that I have already bought Brian's Hotel and got him promotion? Actually I have not completely taken over them yet; I have bought them but left it to the current management for a year or so as transition period. I just have to make sure I do not overspend when I buy this club, developments of grounds and facility and the academy is more important for the future to be secure. I never thought I would ever think of being part of sports in this way, why not, everyone is crazy about it so might as well make money out of their insanity. Or maybe I really do need coffee to wake up from my delusions.

"I am sorry Johann, I don't know how they found out you are here." Colin returns from the kitchen with just my coffee, I guess he knew I was going to tell the goons to bugger off.

"Well you don't read the papers Colin, American billionaire in London in talks to buy Leyton Orient. Such a bizarre story wouldn't have taken long to reach states." I tried taking a sip, but I can still feel the steam on my lips, too hot to be brave with this coffee.

"Why don't you buy Norwich? They have an established fanbase, good workable stadium and facilities, it will only take a bit of sensible investment and a direction to get them to be a great club, and with the talks of new league format coming up it would be a great aquisition."

"Colin."

"And they have such nice kits."

"Colin!"

"Yes."

"I am not overly concerned right now which club I buy; it's a club in London that is up for sale so that's that." The coffee is still scolding hot, might as well put it down.

"That's disappointing. Nevertheless I didn't mean how they found out you were in London, the whole world knows that, I meant how they found out about this place. Everyone thinks you are staying at the hotel you just bought." He looks at me a bit puzzled, but still knowing that I know and I am not troubled by it. He sits himself down, stretching his legs out. He is getting old, even though he is younger than Gilby, he still feels older and more wise at times, certainly more caring. No matter how much I try I can never get angry at him, every time I look at him it makes me smile – I have never met such a warm person in all my life. I guess that is when you know you actually love someone, truly, and I do love him like a son loves his father but is too ashamed to show it.

"Well we have been watched since I got here, and now that I think about it might have something to do with your brother." Yes, it must be Gilbert, why was I thinking it would be my father or the board of directors.

"Hmm interesting …." He ponders over that notion for a bit, while I sit myself down in front of him. "That Berenger fellow is a nice guy though, I mean sure he has the look of someone who has killed a lot of people in war or otherwise, but he is a nice decent bloke, a good person, I can feel that of him,"

"That's what I need to talk to you about. I need a way to distract him and his misfits. There is something I need to do tonight and I cannot have them following me."

"I am sorry but he doesn't swing that way, I already tried. I pretended to go get groceries so I could catch up with you beforehand and warn you, he wouldn't have any of it, told me to stay put straight away."

"You mean you didn't get anything to eat, now that is very disappointing Colin."

"I am sure I can dish something out Johann."

"No its fine, actually that gives me an idea. Order something for tonight and order for our friends as well. Let's relax them up a bit, and why not ask them to come in and have dinner with us. You can tell them I am not well and sleeping it off, I only need to go for half an hour to an hour. Yes that might work."

"Are you sure?"

"Yes, yes. It should work, I don't have much choice. This coffee is good." I finally dare to take a sip, now that it's at perfect temperature, not too hot and not too cold.

My phone rings, I look at it – knowing fully well when that happens you usually pick up the phone. But my thoughts are stuck, my mind is muddled. I pick it up finally at the eighth ring,

"Hello Bill!"

"You took your time, are you out and about?"

"Never mind that, give me the update."

"Well, we went to get the car to scrap, only to find it was not there. Searched it, no car with that registration number exists. We went to the dealer you took the car and driver from, that car and that driver do not and never existed."

"That is very strange."

"Indeed, but that's not all. Not inclined to take no for an answer we applied our methods and all we got out of them was just a bit of nonsensical rambling. Something about it's been fixed by the government, a man with a South African accent, we do not know anything else and we do not want to know anything else."

"Hmmm …."

"I am guessing you know more than me about this, so should I assume it is sorted?"

"Yes Bill, I am sorry to have troubled you with this but yes, let's just leave it at that and assume it's sorted."

"By the way about the other thing you never mentioned the guy you are meeting tonight ..."

"What about it?"

"Do not meet him, it's pointless. Well not pointless for the CIA, they want you do their bidding but keep you away from the real action."

"There is no other way Bill, I have to try."

"You need to trust me more my dear Johann. You will have better luck in Liverpool, I will text you the address."

"How am I supposed to go to Liverpool unnoticed?"

"Who said you have to go unnoticed, your team Leyton Orient is playing Liverpool 3 days from now at Anfield. The club has booked you 5 tickets in the executive section; I told them you would prefer to experience the Kop End. It is easier to slip away from there unnoticed. You have to figure out the rest as and when."

"How did you know ...."

"The South African fellow Berenger O'Brien is a massive Liverpool fan, he would not dare say no. Yes I know who he is, as soon as the car dealer said South African I got my feelers out. He is well known in the Mercenary business, and well known for being a bad Mercenary because of all the right reasons. Go along with it Johann this is the best way. I do not know what you are trying to find out and I do not want to know, but I have this from a very reliable source – Liverpool is your best bet. Better do your research before you get up there, familiarize yourself with the surrounding you are to go into."

"Bill, I don't know how to ..."

"No need Johann, I owe you a lot. You have done more for me than even a brother would do; just promise me that you will be cautious and that you will take care of yourself."

"Of course!"

"And one more thing."

"Yes?"

"If push comes to shove, trust Berenger."

Liverpool it is then, I wonder who his source was, I am not really sure if I want to know. The only way to familiarize myself with the city is to be there. I ask Colin to order extra food for me as well, he looks a bit confused but knows with the smirk I have got that I am up to something – Pizza sounds good Colin – Pizza sounds perfect.

I can hear them all talking and laughing, I was hungry but I don't think I am that hungry anymore. Colin seems to be having a right laugh with them; if Colin approves them then I guess they must be fine. But I just cannot trust anyone right now, they might be sent by Gilbert or by my father or by CIA in disguise who knows. Or maybe Gilbert did send them but how can I know they are not double agents working for my father or CIA or both. I do love pizza though, double pepperoni, perfection. It is such a comforting food. My mother never liked me having junk food; it was always fresh and healthy food for me. I might slip every now and then but it's ingrained in my brain to eat healthy and exercise – keep fit, ready for anything. But I will say it again – I do love pizza. Handmade fresh Italian perfection, this is not junk food this is comfort food, food for the soul.

---

I wake up suddenly not remembering where I am, the last thing I remember was being crowned the pizza king for the entire universe. I think so it is safe to assume that was just a dream. I check my watch, five hours that's all the sleep I could get.

"Ahem, Ahem ….." Who the fuck is that? That made me jump. I look around still trying to open my eyes properly, a man sitting on the side sofa smiling back at me. Probably pleased about sneaking in my room like that beyond all the personal security graciously provided to me and trying his best to look mysterious – all he looks like is a fucking pervert. "Do you like watching people sleep?" I try to sit up a bit; I am not entirely sure what his intentions are, although for all his creepiness he doesn't look like a serial killer type. How would I know even if he was?

"No just you. Pretty boy."

I jump out of the bed in one motion, grab him by his throat and pin him to the sofa. I bet he wasn't expecting that from a pretty boy was he now, "Who the fuck are you?" I say that with intense aggression – I have to admit I think so I spit a bit on his face while asking him that, and I can imagine I just woke up my breath must be rank.

"Calm down Mr Blackmore, calm down. You were supposed to meet me today, you were late by 4 hours I got a tad worried so I dropped by." I still have a grip around his throat; I tighten my grip a bit. "How do I know you are not lying?"

"If you let go I will show you my badge. Who would be crazy enough to take the risk to weasel past Berenger's men, those mercenaries are well known to even the CIA. And ... *cough cough* ..." In a swift move I find myself thrown on the bed with a pinching throat and a throbbing chest. *Cough Cough* it's my turn to gasp for breath now.

"It's not nice is it?" He stands up, brushes his jacket and fixes his tie. "As I was saying Johann, I was waiting for you a while. You were supposed to meet up with me. Or did you just come to England to make your silly investments?"

"Well I decided not to meet up, I was tired." Still nursing my throat, this scroungy dick packs a punch.

"That was not an option. Stop being a child and listen up." He is a nasty character, smartly dressed, square jaw and ratty eyes – the kind you do not want to trust. "Your all mighty dad has a safety deposit in the National Bank, here are the details of it." He hands me a slip with account number and other details. "I would like for you to access that, since you are the only one who has access to it apart from your father. I know it is as surprising to me as it is to you. You will find certain documents in there that we have been looking for and I think it will bring you some closure as well relating to your mother's death. This is the reason why you have been told to come here, so do your bit and piss off back to States. Is that understood?"

"I thought you guys wanted my help."

"We do and that is what the help we need for now, it doesn't mean I have to be nice to you."

"And what are you going to do then?"

"I am going to dig up your dead mother's grave and fuck the shit out of her corpse." I leap for him again, and he punches me hard across my jaw and I fall back to the bed again. He is laughing the most hideous of laughs. "You are too easy to wind up. What I am going to do is CIA's business, nothing for you to be concerned about. You take your posh ass to the bank and do what I have asked you to do. I will contact you to take those documents off you back in States." He comes closer to me grabs my face and to my bemusement kisses me on my lips, "See you later pretty boy." Before I have time to go after him, he climbs off the window like a cat and disappears into the night.

Only twenty minutes gone and already my team, my soon to be team, is two goals down. I don't see them coming back from this, although they show good spirit – seem like fighters, fighters collecting a lot of yellow cards. Maybe it's just unevenly matched teams, seems a lot like it, or maybe I just have too much on my mind to actually get into the game. I do enjoy the experience of being here at the Kop End – the passion and the togetherness; this is a team with proper supporters. I am glad they don't really recognize me as the future owner of Leyton Orient. Mr O'Brien seems to be enjoying himself, two rows down trying to look discreet, with his vigilant friends spread all around, like I am some sort of President, I am my company's in a manner of speaking – just not used to unnecessary security detail. Ah, look at the ginger haired king of the goons jumping up and down now, I bet he has forgotten all about me – discretion down the drain. Never knew he was so much into soccer – fuck it I am going to say soccer you know I mean football anyway – and that also a crazy Liverpool fan by the looks of it. I should have taken more time to size up my carer to be honest, but time is so short I had no choice. I am seriously loosing focus, I wonder why that is. Is it because I thought I saw that journalist? She has been on my mind ever since I saw her at that impromptu press conference. I do not know what it is about her that makes me feel like this. It is a bit similar to what I feel with Galadriel but somehow different – more intense. Maybe I am just not willing to commit and looking for a way out. That's probably what it is; we shall conclude it at that and try to concentrate on the job at hand. I have to get to that address, half time is coming up soon I need to find an escape route. Ah, Leyton Orient scored a goal, perfect timing, tense atmosphere; they all seem distracted – perfect time to make a move.

A major part of the whole city feels utterly deserted; they really love their soccer up here. We were here in the city yesterday, and I did my best to do some sightseeing with my chaperones, I think I roughly know where the address is, but I still don't know what to expect when I get there. Bill told me to meet up with John before heading over to the address. So that is exactly what I am doing. And speak of the devil there he is,

"John, have a seat. Would you like a drink?" I should have explained I went into a cafe, didn't want to be out and about and get spotted. Plus, not really much point in meeting up with someone I don't know in a dark alley.

"Mr Blakemore, with all due respect I will have to say no. And I can't stay long as well." Seems like an odd character, slim, sharp facial features with ears sticking way out. I don't know why I just don't trust people with satellite ears – but then again I don't really trust many people. Something or someone seems to have spooked him. Or maybe he is one of those edgy characters – one more kind of people I don't trust.

"Would you have a seat, at least?"

"I wish I could but I can't. I really do apologize for having wasted your time coming up here and watching some grown up men kick a ball about." I do not like where this is going.

"What can you tell me?"

"I can only confirm your doubt about your father but I cannot give you any proof that is the only bargaining chip I have. Don't worry I will not tell a soul, sir." I really do not like where this is going, he is going to get a right smack across his head soon.

"That is not good enough, how can I persuade you to part with the evidence?" Bill told me that I would get all the information I need at the address which I need to get to soon. What proof does he have? Has he already been to that place and stolen the evidence, but then why would Bill ask me to contact this lunatic for help?

"You can't, it's not worth it, nothing is." The time he has wasted he could have just sat down; people are looking our way, even though they are out of earshot.

"Sit the fuck down." He obliges, I am losing my patience with this insect of a person. "Now, I can give you protection if that is what you need, John."

"No you can't, trust me you can't."

And with that he left, just leaving me sitting there sipping my drink in foolish and confused contemplation. I let him go, I am sure Bill will know how to track him afterwards – and then he would wish he had listened to me.

"Would you like to have something to eat, sir?" A lankly looking waiter, unaware of my boiling emotions, asks me. And before I let my temper get the better of me someone intervenes.

"Yes, we will have two of your specials and two of your creamiest lattes."

"Right away sir," says the waiter and scurries off and sneakily as he came. The guy sits down, and looks at me with a smile that I want to cut the heart out of.

"Berenger O'Brien, I was looking for you everywhere, where were you gone? You know you are supposed to be looking after my well-being?"

"And that's exactly what I am doing." He seems to be holding a lot of emotions back; I guess that is a common trait with soldiery personalities like his. Well at least he got the looks for it that makes him work with calm restraint hardness, although there seems to be so much sadness behind those eyes and yet so much focus. I guess it helps people like him to sleep through the night, with all the things – horrible eventualities they have been made to go through – focus on the mission.

"I don't see you doing that."

"Sir, I might have been sent because of a company directive but I was hired by Gilbert, I owe him more than my life." Why do people hold essential details back, like if you have told me that before we could have worked out a better plan – it's just idiotic. I guessed it but I didn't know for sure. "And besides, you have got a solid lead." He gives it a second, maybe letting it all sink in – I let him have his moment and then he continues, "Liverpool won by the way, barely but still won. I can see why that looney linked you with this team, they have got spirit, ran the big boys ragged. Besides we are in a cosy little restaurant or cafe whatever you want to call it, where no one knows you and are currently awaiting a nice meal and a substandard coffee, how much more looking after do you want?"

"I can do with a slightly more honest company." I sit back looking at him carefully yet with no intention of analysing his facial expression – just looking – trying to size him up.

"In this world, honesty is only relative to the needs of another. But I shall do my best."

"Good, let's just be men today." Bastard is growing on me.

I presume it is getting a bit confusing for you to follow at times, I think one thing but I do another. And I am not usually explaining it before doing it. I apologize for that, even though I do not expect anyone to read this, I still apologize to my non-existent audience.

So let's recap what has happened so far, let's turn this book of live confession into a live soap opera. The note that Galadriel gave me told me to meet one of CIA operative in London who will tell me what I need to do. I had to come up with a valid reason for going to London on such a short notice. So I decided to make enquiries about buying a football club, Leyton Orient was up for sale so I went with that reason. Also I bought a chain of hotels – I don't want to disclose the name, actually you know the name of one where Brian works – that had been going on for a while so it didn't seem like too much of a reason for me to travel to London for and that's why buying a football club came in play. I was then warned by Bill not to meet up with the Agent as it was a trap, I didn't meet him up but he showed up at my flat anyway – creepy fucker. He told me to access a safety deposit in a bank where the missing documents were stored – get them and deliver it to him in States. So what I forgot to mention was that I did go to the bank and got those documents. 'Documents' is a misleading word here – it had just one letter in it. A personal letter written by Hitler to my father, thanking him for his service. It seems authentic enough but a very weak evidence to put such a huge allegation on anyone. Anyway after getting that I decided to follow up on Bill's lead in Liverpool. So I surveyed the city a day before the match, got to know the best route to the address I was supposed to go to. I met up with John before going to the place as Bill suggested but that turned out to be slightly confusing. John seemed to be scared of someone and not willing to part with anything helpful. The annoying part is I do not even know what he was supposed to tell me. He might have the information on the whereabouts of this letter that I already have with me. Anyway Berenger seems to have been tracking me and now I am stuck here with him. Should I trust him enough and disclose about my actual reasons here, or do I keep on sneaking? Somehow I think I should trust him – Gilbert would not have sent him for no reason.

---

Berenger might seem trustworthy but his plan seems slightly sketchy at best. It is now close to midnight and I am to break into a house, and not at the same address as Bill suggested. It is not as if all of a sudden I trust Berenger more than Bill, I just have a feeling Bill's source might have played him unknowingly and Berenger seems a bit more accomplished in the matters of espionage. I have done a fair bit of break-ins in my time but somehow this seems strange, this seems to have a concrete purpose. Now you must be thinking, get real, you have so much wealth that you can just buy the house and waltz in, why would you need to break into someone's home, or probably just hire someone to do it. The fact is I have in the past, out of boredom or a sense of adventure whichever one you want to think about and I don't really care if you believe me or not. I am actually glad that I have done it in the past because now I have an idea how to go about it – this is a job that has to be done by me, what I might find in there is for my eyes only, and that's why I am doing it instead of Berenger or any of his men. I have always been quite a curious person and always wanted to learn new skills. So when I was sixteen or thereabouts, I hired the services of one very interesting individual who taught me all I needed to know about being the perfect uninvited guest. And consequently as part of my training I did a lot of practice runs, obviously I didn't steal anything, I actually left money for them, but it was an interesting trade to learn. Now I am not implying that I am an expert thief or an escape artist but I know enough to do the deed. And it is very useful because, well what if we all got hit by a manic zombie virus, money made redundant and need to break into places for supplies or purely to save my skin from a herd of zombies, without breaking the lock, I know I can do it, can you?

The point is that there is no point. I am just not sure of his plan and I don't completely trust him. That is another reason why I am doing the breaking in myself, I don't even know what kind of proof I will find, if its concrete evidence explicitly linking that old oaf with the dreams of a greater Reich then I do not necessarily want anyone else to see it. I didn't even realize I am already in the house, okay need to focus now, such a shabby house. I can smell a particular dampness, what is that smell?

Okay, I was told I will have at least three hours, O'Brien's men, two of them spotted this guy in a pub and are now drinking with him. I don't really know who the guy is, but we reckon we can get some information out of him and some from this place. And I believe that guy is the keeper of this place. This guy has some sort of connection with that weasel shit I met in the cafe yesterday, and Berenger believes that there are old documents linking my father to the Nazi organization from the times past that has never been seen by the wider world. He also thinks that guy and his associate in the pub are members of the Neo Nazi organization, but they are trying to blackmail my father for these very documents. I have an idea how he knows this, I believe he wasn't just sent here to look after me, I think Berenger and his team had come to this stingy Island for investigative purposes to help me – I guess Gilbert doesn't trust my skills. His men might be blissfully unaware of the gravity of their mission, but he has their trust and they don't seem to question his command.

Let's assume for now that it is the documents that I am looking for, wherever they are in this house they must be well hidden – so let's build an association. So since these guys are with the Neo Nazi organization they would not have reported the authorities and also would not want them to know about it as well. Now the way John was in the cafe, he really made me believe that he had something very concrete, maybe he wasn't sure if I was in with my father or not – but he also tried to distract me away from any sort of evidence being stored in a safe house. There are pictures on the wall, this seems to be the guy they are with at the pub right now, he is old, as old as my father or perhaps even older. There are more pictures of him with his old army buddies, Royal Army, in their uniforms – sneaky. Wait, I just heard something, a tiny gasp; surprise, anger and excitement all combined in one gasp. It came from under me, downstairs; this house has a basement, a hidden basement. I try to locate and find a slight crack in the wooden floor underneath the armchair. I shove my fingers as far down as they would go and try to pull the floor board. It comes off easier than I expected, someone has been down there recently, I take off more floor boards and can finally see steps leading down. I take my gun out and carefully make my way down – Berenger lent me a gun. I walk down the stairs very quietly, they don't creak, very odd. It is dark, as it has been all over the house, but exceptionally dark in here.  I can make out a figure, a womanly figure from a light as if of a candle by that figure, she has long hair, sharply brunette hanging on one side away from the light. Her back is towards me, she is hunched on to a desk. She is holding something in her hands and reading intently – she must have noticed me coming down through all that commotion. I creep up behind her and gently place the gun on the back of her head while grabbing her shoulder lightly just to establish I am in control. "Hand it over," I say as calmly as I can manage.

"I was just looking for the loo." There is some sort of familiarity in her voice, "Is that...? Turn around." It is her, I knew I saw her and it wasn't just my imagination yesterday, what exactly is going on? It is that journalist.

"What are you doing here?" She looks at me with confusion for a minor second and then a grin of acceptance. She shakes off my hand and goes back to whatever consumed her attention. She caresses the papers lying in front of her ever so gently and rides her finger down the open spine of what seems to be a bookkeeper's journal. She finally speaks to me in a whispery giddy voice,

"I came looking for something, and found something far more interesting. Do you want this? Save your daddy of his naughty past?" She looks back at me and then turns her head back before I can answer. I calculate my next words, but what is the point she already knows. I give a sigh deep enough to devour the abyss of endless sorrow.

"My name is Natasha by the way, Natasha Cook."

"Thank you and No! I want it so I can nail the bastard to the grave. It's only that I do not intend to dig my own grave in the process."

"Of course, right." There is a hint of disbelieve in her voice, but I cannot help to feel that she seems dejected and disappointed at the same time.

"I mean it, now kindly hand it over." I try to be as assertive as I can be, but around her I seem to lose all that I was or am, overpowering emotions kneeling me to submit to a will I am unaware of but understand it all too well to have an inkling what it might be.

I hear something else and so does she. The front door of the house, we hear it open, we have to get out of here. It is one thing being rich and powerful but completely another being found out breaking in to an ex Nazi's house. As I look for possible escape routes, Natasha takes me by the hand and guides me out through a secret passage way carved through the inner walls of the basement. It leads down, even further down, to a room, a hidden basement. A basement underneath a basement, filled with all sorts of memorabilia of the horrible war. Documents and files, carefully stacked in a little shelf, not many but enough to establish co-conspirators. This is a danker and darker room, she must have brought those documents up from this room, I can see the gap in the shelf.  This guy is crazier than I thought but why are we here? I look at her and she knows what I am thinking. She leads me through towards the far end of the room, there seems to be a passageway, a small tunnel. After crisscrossing through a complex tunnel system which seems like sewage system we come out on the streets.

"Okay, that was impressive, now may I please have those documents?" Just as I finish saying it, we hear men shouting and running towards us. She runs off and I let her run. With the documents but I let her. I think even she must be shocked with my lack of restraint, I need her trust, I need her, I want her.

"Thanks a lot you buffoons, very discreet." I shout back at Berenger and his loony associates.

"Who was that? Toby, Chris after her, do not let her get away." Berenger seems out of breath.

"Stop! Leave her be."

"Did you find anything at least?"

"Yes and no, let's go home. Our adventures in this city have come to an end. I want to go back and eat Colin's homemade pie."

By the time we get around to calling the dogs at them, they would have removed all of the evidence from this place. There doesn't seem to be any point in that, but I believe she has already recovered the most important part of the evidence we were after.

## ~ (xvii) ~

"How much do you trust O'Brien?"

How much? How can you quantify trust, you either trust someone or you don't. I guess he has a point though, you might trust someone to do something if it meets their end but as soon as it contradicts with their interests that is where true trust lies, I am yet to find someone like that – or have I already found someone and have no knowledge of it.

"Well I found no bugs in the house that might be placed by him, only my own ones. He works in a mysterious way, maybe not so mysterious but enough to not reveal the entirety of his thoughts or schemes before the time is right, I can say the same about your brother." I get back to eating, more vigorously than before, I know there is more to come.

"You have set devices in the house?"

"It is fine Colin, a bit of fooling around near the fireplace is expected – you guys are a lovely couple. Just make sure you do not get too intimate around the things I actually like here."

"Of course sir." His face is blushing red, I have certainly embarrassed the old fool, I shouldn't have. "So how is the battle-born Gilbertous Miraculous?" An interjection of his own making, much appreciated, he is so embarrassed that he is willing to ask about his brother to change the subject.

"He is fine, but he is hiding something from me as am I. I do not know when the time is going to be right for him to part with what he wishes to tell me but I have a feeling it might be all connected to my ongoing escapades."

We take a pause, a long pause, as if contemplating what might be that Gilbert hasn't told me. Although Colin has the look of someone who knows what it is, just not sure when I am supposed to know. I know it is something very personal and something that both of them are scared to tell me – I just wish at least one of them would get it over with, I hate not knowing. But I won't push, I need to be patient otherwise maybe I would not believe it if the timing is not right, maybe that is why they are holding it back – for now I will let it be.

"So what about this Natasha girl, do you trust her?"

"I do not, but something tells me I want to, more than anything."

"Johann, you have that look in your eyes when I just mentioned her, this doesn't seem like the best of ideas." Nothing is a good idea, or a bad idea – it's just an idea until it comes to pass and then the judgement can be made accordingly.

"What look? I am only interested in what she took from me."

"Seems like she took something more than just documents from you."

"O' don't be so corny Colin." Maybe she did, I cannot stop thinking about her.

"It has been more than 3 days and you still haven't stopped talking about her and you do not even know her."

"I need her." I want her; I want to be around her. "I feel something that I cannot understand, and I do not think I want to understand, I want to discover it."

"What about Galadriel? The day you came you couldn't stop talking about her."

"Maybe I need to go back to her, I do not think I am going to find anything else in England anyway."

"Should I pack?"

"I guess so, I will book flight for tomorrow." The damn pie is cold now.

"You don't need to, Gilbert has already sent your private jet over. Your Pilot will be ready to fly you back whenever you are, given we have clearing for flight."

"Hmm .."

"Gilbert said everyone already knows you are here so no point in you cutting down on your luxuries."

"Luxuries …. why not be spoilt for that is what everyone sees me for? So you have heard from him."

"A letter delivered by a messenger doesn't count as hearing from your brother, Johann." There is sadness in his eyes, sadness that yearns to be forgotten – but how can you forget something when it still exists and so do you by remembering it. I turn away and go to my room; there is nothing I can say that would make it better.

I feel like I am going back without achieving anything, just have more confusion than before. That trip to the bank was completely pointless I don't know why CIA were so interested in such a trivial piece of information, something that should already have been established, even without concrete evidence such assumption should already have been established through deduction and there it makes this letter redundant. I don't feel the CIA are serious about exposing my father as a traitor to the country, they are serious about something surrounding him but not exactly that. I am glad that they don't seem that serious about exposing him that keeps me safe and in the driving seat, but it is a bit disturbing to know that they are using me in a way that might blow up on my face without me realizing it which makes me finding concrete evidence even more important – as a fail-safe. Those documents were the only solid lead, well seemed like it I never got to see them so I am not entirely sure if they had anything concrete – concrete, concrete how many times have I used that word already, need to find a better word. Maybe she was just playing with me and there was nothing in them to connect my father with his sins of past. None of the other clues built any conclusive evidence anyway, if there was anything substantial in that basement then I need to know – somehow – I need to know (Conclusive and substantial – better words a lot better than bloody concrete, although I probably have used them before as well). I haven't been able to sleep now for past however many nights, there are so many thoughts racing through my mind and seeing her again did not help matters much. What is about her that enchants me so, why do I feel such a weird connection with her? Berenger wants to stay back and dig out more for me, but I believe that only if he were to know more than I could he do that – something tells me he does. I guess I have taken more time than I was supposed to over here, according to Mister Creepy Agent but who cares, I will go back when it suits me. Anyway I had to wrap things up with Leyton Orient, I guess we will finalize the deal in a later visit. I trust Gilby completely and by association I have chosen to trust Mr Berenger O'Brien, he can hold back all he wants as long as I am eventually the benefactor of his knowledge.

"Hey you!" Brilliant now I have started imagining her, as if my schizophrenia needed another accomplice. I really cannot get her out of my head. It is not that I have forgotten all about Galadriel, I still miss her but this girl is overpowering her scent. She climbs off the window and jumps on the bed, and looks at me – straight in my eyes – I am still confused unable to distinguish if this is just a fantasy or if I have gone completely bonkers, she sits there still staring at me, searching in my hollow eyes for a life that is all too confused and lost beyond recognition, and I am standing beside my bed, why am I standing and not sitting down. It is strange though, if it is some sort of waking fantasy, why is she not wearing something more provocative – knowing the filth that swirls in my mind I am amazed at the simplicity of this thought.

Maybe even my fantasies have given up and gone vapid, although I can smell her scent, sweet nauseating tornado of strawberries whirling around my senses. I know the mind has ways of playing games with its host but this is most irregular.

"Are you going to keep standing there like a creep or will you actually do something?"

What? This doesn't seem like a dream any more, this is real, this is happening now – she is actually here, on my bed – what the fuck do I do?

"I .. youu …" Real smooth as usual.

"Just shut up and kiss me."

And so I do, obey, relieve myself of the responsibility and guilt. I do want her, I have for so long. When I kiss her it feels like an eternal wait inside of me has finally come to an end, is it wrong to do something that feels so good. She pulls me to the bed, taking my shirt off. The touch of her lips onto mine feels like a reality that can only exist in fiction. She pushes me on the bed and get on top of me, she takes her top off while still looking into my eyes which are hollow no more – they are filled with a wonderment that cannot be explained. I touch her bare skin, the warmth awakens a lust inside unknown to me, I do not wish to be separated by that touch.

Something tells me that eventually I will find a way to never be separated no matter what.

And now that it's over and done with, she goes back to her usual self while I am left purring like a little kitten. How can she feel so detached after such a spontaneous intensity?

"Don't take it personally, that was great, but can we get back to business now?" That sounds about right, that's what I get after cheating on someone who cares for me more than I do for her, total detachment. Now I know what women feel when men like her have used and abused them and do not even try to be discreet about it.

"What would that be?" I say without trying to sound hurt, how the hell can she act so normal? What is wrong with her? And why do I still want her more than anything I have ever wanted in my life?

"The documents, remember. You were looking to hide the evidence about your father."

"I wasn't looking to hide, I was looking to expose him in a way that would not compromise myself." She looks at me with a sympathetic look, does she think I feel hurt? She has made it quite clear that this was just a fit of fun for her, or maybe a way of making me vulnerable so she can negotiate to her advantage, I need to play it cool.

"Well the jury is still out on that." I care not to respond, I am already livid with this whole situation and I don't want to

dive into another strong emotion straight away. So I ignore
her remark completely, turn the other way and pretend to go
to sleep. I can see her eyes burning a hole at the back of my
neck, trying to read me, see if I am not wounded and why
would I be? For her I am a rich bastard with a lot to waste
without a care in the world, given a silver spoon and have
never had to lift a finger for anything in my life, I probably do
this sort of thing with a lot of my other good looking
associates. I cannot say I have never used someone myself
before, but I do not appreciate being done over, it's not a
nice feeling to say the least. I can still sense her looking at
me.

"What exactly are you doing Johann?" There is a hint of
frustration in her voice, she wants confrontation.

"What does it look like? It's late and I am tired. I have a flight
to take tomorrow. I am going to sleep. You can do the same if
you want, or use the window to go wherever else you fancy.
We can talk about 'the business' tomorrow, as long as you
have those documents in a safe place – I do not see the point
of discussing about it for now." I turn my head around and
look at her looking at me. She seems disappointed, that look
is so familiar. My mother used to give me that look whenever
I was unable to tell her the undertone of Keat's essence in
one of his works accurately. It is a similar look, although this
time the disappointment is mutual. "If you do not feel like
sharing the bed you are more than welcome to use the sofa,
it is unusually comfortable. There are extra blankets and
pillows in the wardrobe if you want." She looks over at the

sofa and then at the wardrobe, she is thinking about it. She looks so sublime, that smooth glistening skin and those perky breasts hidden by her long curly hair which she has dyed a subtle shade of amber. I know she has dyed them because the first time we met her hair were as black as my mother's used to be, and it looked more natural on her than this shade, although I prefer the amber it matches her fiery nature. "Or not, either way, I am off to sleep. Goodnight." I can hear her brain working, trying to make sense of my reaction. After a while of pretending to go to sleep, I fall asleep.

I wake up in the morning, or what I think is the morning, alone. She is gone, as I would have expected her to have been. A file left by the bedside, I take it and open it. As my eyes adjust to being awake, I realize these are the documents she took from that basement. There is a ledger by the file as well, but it is not original, come to think of it the documents don't seem original. All are a copy, I guess she took the original with her, smart girl.

I call out for Colin, the door opens slightly, "Quit calling for your man slave and join me for breakfast sleepyhead." So she didn't leave, breakfast, must still be morning. I put my gown on and walk out to the dining area. Something smells delicious.

"You shouldn't have gone through all that effort for me." I realize how hungry I am now.

"As much as I would like to take the credit for it, actually Colin fixed this up. He went to the market to get something for you, for the journey I think. He said something along the lines 'Johann needs it for his journey' - whatever that might be."

"M&M's and a book by an unknown to me author."

"What's that?"

I sit myself down, and make myself a plate. "Hmm nothing, just mumbling. So you met Colin? What was that like?"

"It's not the first time I have met him, but it might be the first time he trusted me." Nice, so both brothers like keeping secrets from me. I carry on eating my breakfast.

"You don't care about that? How odd. Either you are really hungry, or still slightly bitchy about yesterday, or really don't care."

I look at her, while eating, and try to think why she is trying to get under my skin. This between us is morphing into something completely different. There is bitterness, but not out of spite. I carry on eating.

"Fine, be like that, business then. As you would have already noticed, I have left you a copy of the ledger and the documents. The originals, well they are in a secure location. But these on their own are nothing; we need to make connection and someone that brings sense to that connection."

"And what do you suggest?" Still eating, and sipping on orange juice without pulp – I do love Colin.

"Well I need to go to Berlin, I believe I will find out more over there." I just realized, I do not know why it took me so long to realize, she is naked. Did she – was she when I came out for breakfast? I am seriously confused what is going on. Should I say something? She must have been naked all this time, because there are no clothes around here. Did she talk with Colin like that? I know he is gay, but that's just weird. Good thing, Berenger and his boys are not around, or did she already know that? I haven't a clue what is going on in my life do I?

"What are you thinking about?"

"Oh nothing, just wondering what you want me to do while you are off having an adventure in Berlin?" I try to look away, but now all I can see is her – and I think someone else has started waking up under this gown. She is beyond perfection.

"Don't talk with the CIA, and if you have to just leave me out of your conversations."

"How do you …." How does she know that CIA is keeping tabs on me?

"I know, just leave it at that. Now can you tell me what you were actually thinking about?"

I put my fork and knife down, just to be careful, I really want something to happen but I don't want to seem like I want to make it happen. "Well, I was just wondering why you are naked."

"Why? You do not like what you see."

"I do like what I see, very much. But that's not my point, you know what I mean." She walks over towards me, slowly, keeping a constant eye contact. I am entranced and I do not want to disrupt what might happen. She bends over, her breasts nesting my chest, caressing ever so slightly, and she whispers in my ear 'I just wanted to wake up both of you' and runs her fingers down my torso to my balls. Gently, ever so gently nudges it upwards, her lip touching mine – I look into her eyes – such perfection, and as she discreetly lets me in 'Something to remember me by' I think to myself that there cannot be anything in this world to make me forget anything about her.

*'The apocalyptic nature of human reality dictates that its existence is in parallel to the development of its intellect. By the rate of its determination the end is surely nigh for those who choose to cling to a hope that was never meant to sustain the intellect.*

*God in his creation was a manifestation of a deranged messiah, wanting something different than his mundane existence. Religion is the degradation of human essence, it subsides the basic nature of survival, the basic instincts of survival by giving a fruitful outcome, a reward, heaven, for giving up. It is a creation of a coward, who got tired of surviving.*

*If the world is to end tomorrow, humans are not to accept it as the will of God, they are supposed to fight it and see a way past it, make sure tomorrow still survives. If there was actually a God and a religion to follow, humans would have gone extinct centuries ago, one by one from every part of the world. There have been numerous eventualities to exhibit the end of the world, but we have seen them all through by believing in ourselves more than anything.*

*There is no Heaven and there is no Hell and there is certainly no God, no one is waiting for us on the other side. What is there for sure is – us – and our need to survive for as long as possible and the will to pass the same need to the next generation. We are still here because we are determined to be here, if it were up to a God we would all be in Heaven right now and how boring would that be, some place so remote to our reality, bereft of imperfections, so inhuman. Believe in yourself; believe in your intellect – before you believe in anything or anyone else.'*

I think I understand, and I believe I can relate to it. So high up in the clouds, I am glad of reading something to make me ponder – truly in depth.  Another passage reads,

*'Progressive values of a human mind are a product of logic and reason applied to their very core with the sensibility of human emotions. And as such they come from unencumbered thoughtful prognosis within a defined societal framework – not from unexplained divine entities or from outdated books that strive to pigeon-hole our existence into extinction.'*

It is a wonder how I have never come across this author before, there is so much truth in what he writes, although leaves a lot to explain but those are the parts that make you think. I need to find him and have a conversation with him one day, I feel as if I have known him all my life, but only now realize that he has been a part of me all this time. What's his name again, Momus Najmi, the book titled, 'Intercepting Convictions through Contradictory Perceptions.'

Although as riveting as this is, I still find myself thinking about her in the little pauses of my thoughts.  I do not think I have ever experienced such a connection on a physical level with anyone before, purely animalistic yet a telepathic compassion that is only reserved for higher beings not yet imagined. It was perfect moment, yet I do not think a perfect goodbye. From the shadows she came and thus she returned. I have no idea when I will see her again or if I will ever see her again.

*'Variations of mental awareness within oneself limits their ability to deliver a truer prognosis of emotional confession – the one who delivers never has full control over their limitations and the one who receives does not understand the limitations of the deliverer. As the one who delivers struggles unknowingly in this process so does the one who receives impaired through their limitations to receive a truer picture of emotions swimming in the diversity of their own mental perceptions.'*

*'She is drowning, I can see her face. Something is wrong with her legs, she cannot get up. She is calling out to me – screaming, I can see her screaming but I cannot hear her screaming. I cannot move, I cannot reach her – I am trying to say something but nothing is coming out of my throat. There is water coming out of my throat now, it drops to my hands and now it turns into blood. I am drowning in my own blood.'*

I open my eyes to sunlight shimmering on my face, trying to tear in my mind, shaking my conscience. That was a new variation to my nightmares, myself bleeding. I feel as ever that my dreams are trying to tell me something, but so far nothing makes sense to me. Maybe it is the acts of my father haunting me subconsciously mixed with the guilt for my mother's death. Whatever it maybe, I am actually glad for the rude awakening by Gilbert today.

"Are you ready to wake up?" a deep voice calls out to me with hidden anger and utter disappointment – much like my own monologue of late. He looks at me for a brief moment while tugging the rest of the curtains on the side to let the bright sun roar down at me with its might once again as it does every morn, wonder what has made him so unpleasant towards me.

"Depends if I have a reason to wake up Gilby." I try to keep my grin to myself but as ever fail miserably.

"Are eggs and bacon enough of a reason?" He says while setting them down on the breakfast table by the window.

"Good as any, I would say," I get out of my bed, unclothed as ever put my robe on and sit down to eat – I didn't realize how hungry I was, I rarely do till I actually sit down to eat and recently it has been a regular occurrence. I look up at Gilbert looking at me, "Are you not going to join me?"

"Depends if there is a reason to do so." A slight smirk escapes his face. "Is a tale of mischief and mayhem enough of a reason?"

"As good as any." We both burst into laughter. "It is good to have you back Johann, I was really worried about you. Would a phone call have hurt? So what did you discover? Or whom did you discover, I should ask?" The sun is high up in the sky, feels late morning or close to noon – I think it is afternoon; I just slept in since I came back from my flight so late anyway.

"Whom? Nothing escapes you does it. I knew there was a reason behind the abrupt awakening." I say while eating – I really am hungry – nothing better than crispy bacon.

"Do you think it is wise doing that just weeks before your engagement?" He looks at me vacantly while sipping his orange juice. Obviously he is having his lunch – a standard sandwich with orange juice. I love the smell of his sandwiches, always fresh with the perfect combination, I used to eat half of his when I was a kid, that was such a long time ago. Fresh bread, tomato and chilli chutney, slice of ham slightly grilled, two thin slices of tomatoes, lettuce, avocado and cress, and to top it off thin slice of grilled chicken – that is one hell of a sandwich. Always ate it with crisps, maybe it's an English thing, they do love their crisps there.

"To be honest, I wasn't really thinking about that or anything for that matter." I say taking a momentary break from gulping down a humongous helping of eggs. "I suppose not."

"Now what is that supposed to mean," a bit of egg sprays out of my mouth as I say that – maybe I should have waited to swallow it before I said anything.

"You never think before you act, always follow your heart or should I say your dick in this instance. Your actions carry more weight than you credit them for, Johann." He slides my coffee nearer to me as if suggesting for me to slow down, I take a sip of the coffee accepting that maybe I should slow down a bit – subtle, very subtle.  "A lot of people are depending on you to run this company in the future and this engagement of convenience is vital to it."

"You would find Gilbert that it is not mine but someone else's devious actions that carry more weight." I know he is right, but I also know he is wrong. Natasha was not a lustful decision; there is something between us that I cannot explain and no matter how much I try to convince myself I cannot turn away from it.

He falls silent for a bit, looking at his hands. Should I tell him what I found or should I wait? Or does he already know?

"Well, whatever you found I hope it helps to give you some peace and make you realize your own worth in this world." I will wait, now doesn't seem the best of time. "I hope so too." He gets up and leaves, takes the tray with him leaving me my coffee and half his sandwich.

---

Phone rings, "Hello!", "Johann" - I take a second - "Galadriel". "How many times do I have to tell you to call me Gladys instead?" "But how can I call my elf queen anything other than her true name." "Oh Shut up."

"I am glad you are back, I want to see you. Can we go for dinner tonight?"

"I am not sure if I want to go out in public today that whole football club business isn't going to fade away soon."

"Okay well, maybe I can come over then and you can have your amazing chefs cook something nice for me." "Deal"

"I will see you in the evening," "See you."

And now the real guilt kicks in. I have never planned to like her, I always thought I would go through with the engagement, reveal my father's hideous nature and then call off the wedding and obviously take control of the company. To be honest, I do not really need Mr Wilkinson's company – Galadriel can run her father's company by herself – but I seem to have grown attached to her.  This love malarkey is really confusing.

Evening, I hate it when people make plans like that. I mean tell me a particular time – how will I know which part of evening do you mean. I see a shadow lurking by outside my room, "Who is it?"

"O' Sorry sir, I was just wondering if you are ready for your back to business updates."

"Sebastian, it's you. Come on in, don't wait outside, you should have knocked."

He comes in, with a sense of confusion about him, "Why are you being so nice to me?"

"Whatever do you mean; I am always nice to you."

"Yes, but not in this fake tone."

"Okay fine, you got me. I need a favour." I need to get my hands on that letter that my father was so worried about while reading. And also consulting the doctors afterwards, I still hope he has cancer and dying soon. I cannot get it myself, he keeps his study locked and at this point if I do anything my intentions will be revealed and he might be on guard.

"Is it about that letter your father received from Munich before your adventure to London?" Now I look confused, how the hell did he know?

"How the …."

"It is okay; don't worry, Berenger told me to help you in your pursuit in whatever way possible."

"You of all people, the world never ceases to amaze me."

"Mr Blakemore, I know what you are trying to uncover, and it is fairly dangerous. If the CIA even gets the whiff of what you are trying to do, your life might be in great danger – not to think about what will happen if your father really is one of them. What will he do to you, or me, or even Gilbert?"

"Okay calm down, Berenger should never have involved you into this mess. You are not the type; I will find another way of getting hold of that letter. And please seriously Sebastian, I been telling you for 5 years now just call me Johann."

"That is not what I meant. I have already made copies of the letter; I have kept it safe in my locker in the company building. To be honest it isn't much of a clue, cannot make any sense of it – just travel arrangements. I will go and get it for you – I should be back by evening." Again with the bloody evening – why cannot people be more precise?

"I am not sure about today, I am supposed to have dinner with Gladys sometime in the evening at home. I have to make arrangements for that as well. Should go and talk to the kitchen staff actually."

"It is all arranged for, Gilbert told me about it. I have had the house staff arrange a nice romantic dinner for you in the garden – alfresco style. I guess he is a bit pissed off at you right now, but I don't judge – heart wants what the heart wants. I will leave the letter in the top drawer of the desk in your study. I have taken one key with me; just make sure to keep it locked."

"Why not just put in on my bedside drawer?"

"If the dinner turns out to be as romantic as I told the staff to make it, you might be reaching for something else in your bedside drawer at night. Not wise to spoil such a moment now is it."

"You really have thought about everything." He really is a good person, a very clever one at that, fiercely loyal to me and a big reason why I should not involve him into this anymore.

"What about back to business updates then?"

"Well, not much at the moment. Profits are still steady, your father rarely shows up for board meetings anymore and since he doesn't really lay down a strategy as such the board has been following your strategies in his absence. I have been conveying them the plan so far. They are not really bought out with this whole plan of marriage and merger. Wilkinson Corporation will be launching the new line of their cars soon – the plan is being carried out without the board's knowledge, it is best if they don't know even though, if they did know I suspect they actually would be glad you are trying to take over the company this way then through marriage. We will see what happens when the time is right."

"Good, about this soccer club."

"Yes, what were you thinking, it will take a lot to bring a club like Leyton Orient back into profitable zone. I know it is a private acquisition for you, but the board is really iffy about this move of yours, they think you are getting distracted."

"I don't know, I am not an expert on soccer. Can you convey a message to the board from me about the club?"

"I suggest you do it in person, your father has been away for a while and is planning to fly out to Argentina tomorrow. They want one of the Blakemore to actually communicate with them in person."

"South America? Okay fine, set up a meeting for tomorrow."

"I already did that, I was just hoping you would say yes to it, is afternoon fine for you?"

"What time Sebastian, be slightly more specific?"

"Half past two in the afternoon?"

"Perfect. That will do. You will be attending that meeting with me."

"Of course, sir."

Almost evening, still waiting for her – I am a bit anxious. I want to just tell her that I have been with Natasha – although I am not sure what it meant. I guess I am being a bit selfish, I want to keep both – but right now I do not know if I have either one.

I guess you must be wondering, what my plans might be for this possible takeover or merger depending it pans out. It is just secondary to this monologue, I can let the great mystery play itself out – but being completely honest I really cannot be bothered so I will summarize it for you.

Remember the deal I was told to do, the big merger – this all connects to it. My father wants me to get married as you know, to Galadriel Wilkinson, whose father owns the Wilkinson Corporation. Now Mr Marcus David Wilkinson is as shrewd and evil minded of a business man as they come. And my father and him are the best of friends – peas in a pod. They both want to merge the company, but they want to do it the old fashion way by marrying their only children to each other, who will both be equal owners of the same merged company. On the offset it seems like a brilliant idea, my father wants to make our company even richer than it already is and then hand it over to me and Galadriel. You might now think I am being ungrateful – Nazi or not that's a very noble sentiment. Obviously, it would be so much easier if I shared his ideologies – which is why this whole thing doesn't make sense to me. I had high suspicion before, but now after viewing those documents Natasha and I uncovered I am fairly certain, I never mentioned it to Natasha, but my father and Mr Wilkinson seem to be the prime movers in the whole secret Nazi operation before and right now. Wilkinson's company, owns and operates most of the oil rigs in Northern America and has now decided to go into car manufacturing. Our company deals mostly in weapon manufacturing and pharmaceuticals – I know weapons and pharmas don't make sense but maybe they are starting to now. If these two companies are combined, which are not competitors by any measure, they can take down most competing companies in America. A company like that can influence a lot of policies on government level – whether it is in this country or any other. We shut down most of our operations in Europe and it would seem we are actually not looking to expand or gain influence but to reduce influence – that could not be far from the truth. Those businesses were sold off to subsidiary companies – they are still within reach, but this gives both companies the opportunity to concentrate more on a single region that can produce the most influence throughout the world. And those subsidiaries can work to increase our influence, same narrative perpetuating from a different voice coming from the same rotten throat. And this is why I am so opposed to the entire merger.

I am actually interested in Wilkinson's new car project, unknowingly his company has two of the brightest minds in robotics who I am after – I envision a future of AI and I think those two will be prime commodities in the future. I have already made offers to both of them, and with their help, the cars being manufactured right now will be a complete disaster whose effect will take place within first month of the initial sales in America. And once their first ever cars fail – their reputation would be completely tarnished. That way I can suggest to our good friend Wilkinson to let Blakemore takeover this department before the merger so we can help save face in the market – doesn't matter as both companies will be one in the future anyway. That is the only part of their company I want to keep a hold on, oil is a thing of the past there is no future in there.

And now you must be thinking, but one way or another these two companies will be merged anyway so what is the whole point of this exercise. I am not so sure at the moment, I believe everything will fall in its place once it takes motion. There is supposed to be a long gap between our engagement and actual marriage – I am sure our fathers will propose to have our wedding at the exact same time when the deal can be finalized for dramatic effect – I suspect I will have more than a year or two to figure everything out, till that time I will have their car manufacturing side transferred over to us for half the value and the two brilliant scientists to help me take a complete different direction for Blakemore Industries.

And please seriously do not ask me about this club that I bought. I am not really sure if I can pull out of that now – otherwise I really will not be able to explain my reason for being in London to a lot of people. I guess I will just have to run a football club, maybe make it be profitable, open up a sports management department and transfer it over to the company – probably buy one or two more clubs elsewhere in the world to make it believable. Actually that is not really a bad idea, there is a lot of money in sports. And I think I have thought on those lines before as well.

'Knock, knock'

"Yes?"

'Knock, knock, knock'

"Yes, come in"

'Knock, knock, knock, knock'

"Who the fuck is it?" I walk over to my home office door, adjacent to my bedroom and my private library. And in walks that horrible despicable person.

"Hello sweetheart, you took your time."

"Could have just come in you fuckwit."

"O' testy are we today."

"I thought we were supposed to set up a meeting somewhere in a dark and dingy place."

"You would have liked that now wouldn't you pretty boy."

"What the fuck do you want?"

"As much as I would like to waggle your tail, give me the file you retrieved from the safe deposit so I can be on my way."

I walk over to my desk, unlock the second drawer and get the letter out from the false drawer inside and hand it over to him. 'Not much of a file, just a pointless letter."

"We will determine how pointless it is when the time is right, you just be a good boy and do what you are told." How the hell did he even get in? Who let him in? I really need to update the security in this place it feels at times living in a fucking hotel, anyone can walk in whenever they want.

"By the way I met your Scouse friend, John."

"Who?"

"You know John, he had a big gaping wound from his right ear to the left?"

"What are you talking about?"

"O' yes that's right, I did that to him after your coffee house chat with that toad. I can do a lot worse to people than just agonizingly kill them, remember that next time you try to fool us and hop on your own, pretty boy." He turns and leaves, with my standing there like an idiot without a response. I pour a glass of scotch and down it. Does everyone know everything? What the fuck is going on?

They have really gone to a lot of effort with this whole dinner, I do not know what they were told but it seems like I am trying to win over the love of my life. Strange, the effort seemingly I am making for her – that she thinks I am making for her – but on my own I would have never even thought about doing something like this. Our table is under a tree, far end of the garden, the branches of the tree are lit with small delicate lights which are giving the effect of stars fallen to the ground, candles on the table. There is some music playing, I don't know where but I can hear it. It is not loud enough to disrupt the conversation, just mildly playing in the background – I love this piece I have heard it before, seems so familiar, but I do not know who is it by.

"Johann this is so beautiful, I didn't expect this. It is better than going out."

"Well now you know why I prefer staying in." I take a sip of wine, such perfectly balanced wine. I have always been fond of wine, I am no wine connoisseur but I do know a good wine when I taste it. She looks very, how should I put it, provocative. That dress of hers, hugging each curve of her slender shaped body, revealing her ample breasts just ever so slightly to entice the imagination – I want to rip it all apart and examine her more thoroughly. What is it with both these women that make me go so wild?

Dinner is served, fourteen small dishes of delight one after the other. We almost eat in silence, maybe the food is too delicious to spoil it with conversation or perhaps there is something bothering both of us and we do not know how to bring it up. So instead we have decided to concentrate on the food and not our emotions. I know what is bothering me, I can feel the guilt – it is a bit over powering and I am conflicted like I have never been before.

"What is it Johann, what are you thinking about?" You really don't want to know. I am thinking about my guilt for cheating on you and at the same time about ravishing you.

"Oh nothing, just a bit tired. And really full from that amazing dinner. I really cannot take the credit for it. My chefs are just amazing."

"Yes they are, but they would not have done anything unless you would have told them to. It is the thought that counts." Okay fine, I will take the credit for it.

"Why don't we go for a bit of a walk? There seems to be a lit pathway into the woods." I really didn't notice that till she pointed it out. There are small specks of lights on the trees and the grass, lighting a path for a romantic walk. This is really neat, the woods behind our mansion obviously belongs to us. It is acres upon acres of land, somewhere close to seven hundred acres or more. It is easy to get lost over here; I mean these woods have their own wildlife, nothing too wild though we got rid of any overly dangerous animals. There is river that flows by the middle of the forest, ends up in a cave – I used to go there a lot when I was a kid. There is a lake as well, not a natural one, my father had it made. It is actually really beautiful, and it would be even more beautiful if that wasn't the very lake where my mother drowned.

"So I will be travelling for around two weeks to a month. I hope you will be fine. I am actually going to Argentina. We have some properties over there, so need to take care of a bit of business." Argentina, who else was going to Argentina?

"When are you going?"

"Actually my flight is for tomorrow that is why I wanted to meet up today before I left." I am not her keeper or anything, but I have a feeling this is all of a sudden plan – otherwise she would have mentioned it before. "That's fine; bring me something nice from Argentina."

We keep on walking slowly, hand in hand, along the path built for us. Just walking silently, with the sounds of the night and hooting of the owls, there is no need to talk – absolute serenity. After a good half an hour walk into this pathway – I know a lot of bloody lights – we end up in a bit of a clearing. There is a mat, picnic blanket, laid out in the middle, with more wine on the side, and there is a bonfire lit. We walk slowly towards it and sit down on the mat. She looks towards me and says, 'You know, I have never done it in the forest under the stars." I let out a cheeky smile and say, 'Well, what are we waiting for then."

The passion of the wilderness flows through us, as I slip my hand under her dress and caress her tender skin. She reaches for my lips and kisses me gently, waits for a second or two just looking into my eyes, and then kisses me again this time with more vigour than I have ever been kissed with before. The sensation of openness in between the elements, yet seclusion is overwhelming. And under the starlight, I dive into the abyss of momentary bliss and do it gladly. The panting and the breathing is all the sounds I can hear – and so I travel into the non-remembrance of events – knowing and remembering all yet nothing that can be revealed.

I don't know when I fell asleep looking at the stars, with her head resting on my shoulder, but now that I have woken up it seems early morning, close to dawn. The bonfire has been put out, and there seems to be no sign of her about. I get up, collect my things and start the walk back to the house. Hopefully Sebastian brought that letter back for me by now. I feel hungry, I am ravishing, what an experience that was last night, what will I do about Galadriel, I wonder.

I stumble back to my room and go to my study adjacent to my room, linking both of them. I find a lot of letters on my desk, put in a neat pile on one side. The stories for this month from the orphanage, I still do not have time for this – why can Gilbert not understand that? I am going to give scholarships for their further education to all of them anyway. I find the letter, in my first drawer; he didn't even lock the drawer. Talking about it not being secure and what not, then goes and places a secretive copy of the letter unlocked. I sit down behind the desk, and think, if I want to have breakfast now or sleep for a bit longer and then have breakfast.

Anyway, let's open the envelope. It feels like there is more than a letter in here – yes, there is a letter and two tickets, return tickets, to Argentina – obviously copies of the tickets and not the original ones. I say it's not a letter, it is barely a note – this doesn't make sense.

*'The travel arrangements from our end has been made for the funeral, please give confirmation of your plans to us in advance so we can prepare for any other eventualities. We have acquired from our resources that you and your travelling companion are under surveillance and as such we would advise you to proceed with caution. It is best to travel separately.'*

That doesn't make sense; this note is nothing to be so worried about. I mean he must know that he is being watched. Argentina – didn't Gladys said something on the lines of … and what would you know. The second return ticket is in her name, so she is going to Argentina with him. There can be a number of explanations but the obvious one would be that she is working with him and her father. She knows, and she is in on it. Maybe that is why they want to merge the company, so after marriage she can get rid of me- permanently – and then run the company. Now I really don't know what to do with her, I am to be engaged with her. Although it still doesn't explain his reaction after receiving this letter, is there a hidden message in this note. Or maybe it is this other letter that is in here, I really need to look at things properly. Okay now it makes a bit more sense.

*'Dear Brother,*

*As we reach our final stage, I regret to inform you that my health is failing me. I don't think I can live beyond a month. I know the doctors before gave me 5 more years, but for some reason my decline has been accelerated.*

*I hope my daughter is keeping you company, and helping your misguided son to come to an understanding. She is the future for what we want to achieve, remember that.*

*I'll advise you to quicken our plans, and get the engagement and marriage done with, then finally our families can be united together, and we can be truer brothers. The CIA suspects, as they have been for the past 50 or so years, they might have someone close to us again to spy and collect information.*

*You must get this done as quickly as you can. I will live out the rest of my wondrous life here in Argentina, there will be a small funeral, and make sure to come say your goodbyes. My company will be run under the impression that I am still alive, it has officially been passed on to Galadriel but it will take some time for all to be in place – let her deal with those side of proceedings.*

*And as ever, I am shamefully sorry about Klaudia. I know you do not like old wounds to be opened, but I gave into base desires and did not think it through. It was my fault, although through such actions we discovered her to be a mole and drowned her insolence – still I broke your trust as a friend and I regret it to this day.*

*I might have drawn my last breathe till you get this letter, so I want to wish you all the best for restoring the Reich and making it even stronger than it had ever been. Our vision will succeed one way or another the righteous will always prevail.*

*Yours Sincerely,*

*Marcus*

This is too much to take in, I think I will go to sleep first and then have breakfast. Off to bed – hello nightmares.

~ (xxv) ~

*'Mother … mother …. she cannot hear me under water, she is drowning I try to reach for her but she is so far away from me. A moment ago I was in her arms and now she is a fair distance away and the more I try to reach for her the further she is pushed. I hear a voice shouting down at me, it's a wolf, big and ugly and its shouting at me, "you killed your spy mother, you little bastard." I cannot breath, I just want my mother to hold me again. I cannot breath.'*

I wake up sweating, and screaming out for my mother. There are choices we can make, we are told. We are free to choose as we please, free. But are we really and can we really choose? Choice is an illusion given to us to make us believe that there is any freedom involved in our lives. And this illusion does become a reality when we spring the thought into existence by believing in it but the freedom of its undertaking still remains an illusion. We live in a world where we are controlled by the thought of our freedom, we are free, free enough to cage ourselves in the illusion of freedom. An absolute waste of intellect.

He knows there is something wrong, he knows I know more than I should. But he will not come out to face me yet. He will hide in plain sight – my patience in running thin. It would be easier if he just confessed, why must he persist on dragging this charade. For years and years, I thought my mother died because of my stupidity, trying to save me from drowning in that lake. That is what that monster told me again and again, that is what everyone told me. Maybe not in the same vehement manner as my father, a different version but same conclusion, she died trying to save me. But now if I read that letter right, there might be a different version to that story – maybe she did not drown, but was made to drown. I knew it, that he killed her or got her killed. I just never had it confirmed and everyone told me a different story including Gilbert – she drowned trying to save me. And that's what I have been telling myself for so long.

I remember that day still in my own way, a lot is blurry from that memory but I can see her face drowning, the look of saddened love on her face as she looked at me for the last time before she went under forever. They took her body out and buried her by the great oak tree we used to play around – but for me she is still there in that lake, telling me it's okay it is not my fault. I never believed her and even now I am not sure if I do. I know in some way it was my fault, maybe not what I did, but my existence itself was at fault and the cause of her death. The story ran in the newspapers all over the country,

*'Blakemore Olympian beauty drowned in the family lake. Mrs Blakemore, found dead in the lake while enjoying a picnic with her son. Johann Blakemore suffered a heatstroke while floating on an inflatable boat and fell in the lake. Klaudia went in to save her son, she managed to get Johann back on the inflatable boat, unfortunately got caught up in ropes and nettings under water from the time of the lake's construction. Once an Olympic Bronze Medallist, could not swim to save her life as her son watched his mother drown in bewildering horror.'*

That day has always been hazy in my mind, I remember the sun was shining bright, although I had been in the lake with the sun even warmer than that day and still not suffered with heatstroke. I was old enough to understand a lot of things, but the grief of losing your mother right in front of your eyes and being shunned by everyone as the reason for her death can do terrible things to one's mind. I was only 10, still coming to terms with the way our world works and trying to determine my own purpose in it – I am nearing thirty now and still the purpose eludes me.

## ~ (xxvi) ~

I want to strangle him with my own hands and watch the life squeeze out of him, till his eyes pop out. There is nothing in this world I hate more than sharing the same genes as the monster that killed my mother. And all of those people who lied are just as guilty, all of them, Gilbert, he has been lying to me all my life. Maybe he was told the same lie, but for some reason I doubt it. He was the one who took me away from the lake – he must have known, is he involved in her death? Is that the guilt that gnaws at him and cannot talk to me about it?

But for all my hatred there is still one nagging thought left, a minor observation which is becoming a major pain and something that might make me adjust my plans. The documents that we discovered, even the detailed ledger, does not directly implicate my father. The mention of his name is there, but as a facilitator of sorts, which can be easily denied and disregarded by the court of law. It doesn't really show his actions had the intentions that anyone might want to incriminate him against. Secretly, I am relieved that to be the case. I want to confront him for his heinous actions but don't necessarily want the world to know that – like I mentioned before I carry his name, and I really do not wish to be dragged in mud no matter what he did. A yarn needs to be spun to bewitch the CIA and retain my fortune while witnessing the monster's demise.

"Excuse me sir, your breakfast. You wanted it in your study. I hope it is okay." A shy young girl, probably in her early twenties pokes her head in the study after knocking gently on the door. I look up at her and give her a smile, still holding the letter in my hand having re-read it a million times, point her to put it on the table. She is the new girl in the kitchen, for the life of me I cannot really remember her name and to be honest I cannot be bothered. No this is not going to lead to where you think this is leading to; I don't just have my way with all the members of the household or otherwise. "Thank you, that is absolutely fine." I go back to my letters, she lingers for a second longer than she is supposed to and then leaves.

I am supposed to get engaged with a person in two months' time who is even more deceitful than my father. I really don't know at the moment how I want to play this; mischief is afoot and demands the trickster to play the fiddle.

I pick up my phone and ring Sebastian, answers within two rings. "Hello sir, is everything fine?"

"Yes, everything is fine. Listen, can you come pick me up yourself for the meeting? I need to catch up on few details before I talk with the board."

"Of course, I will be around your place in an hour."

"Good!"

There is a gentle knock at my door again, "It's Samantha."

O' so the new chef's name is Samantha, I know all my chefs, they are great fun but her shy friendliness is slightly unnerving to me – maybe because she is actually quite cute. "Yes, Samantha, I am not really done yet." Actually come to think of it, I haven't even started eating. "Oh no it's not that, I am sorry to bother you again and again, but I forgot to give you this letter. It came in the post today and I was supposed to give it to you with your breakfast. Well I say post, there was a guy in a suit who hand delivered it and asked me to give it to you as soon as possible. I didn't want to disturb you while you were sleeping so I thought I would give it to you with your late breakfast and then I forgot. I am sorry I am just blabbering on, here is your letter any way, weird black envelope, I like black envelopes, I think they are cool, if that is the kind of thing you like. I am not implying that you like that sort of things or that there is anything wrong with liking such thing. Anyway here you are." She hands it to me and then looks at me intently as if expecting some form of accolade for delivering a letter.

"Yeah black envelopes are cool. Well its fine nothing to worry about, thank you for actually not disturbing me while I was sleeping."

"Do you not like your breakfast? Would you like me to make you something else? I know Mr Pohl usually has only Simon make your food but Simon wasn't feeling well and I couldn't find Mr Pohl anywhere so I just made what I thought you might like." I cannot believe I am having this unnecessary conversation.

"What's wrong with Simon?"

"He has a bit of a problem with his back, it is to do with his age but he doesn't rest, never listens."

"Yes, he can be a bit stubborn. Well I am sure I am going to like whatever you have made, and make sure you cook something nice for Simon as well so he feels better. Let me know how he is feeling later."

"Of course I will, okay I will leave you to it and come a bit later to get the tray."

"Thank you."

Where has he gone off to, Mr Gilbert Pohl? And these fucking black envelopes, that is exactly what I need right now, CIA breathing down my neck. That creep just met me yesterday, what more does he want? I guess it will have to wait whether they like it or not, I have got better things to do at the moment.

"Johann, are you okay?" I come back from my deep thinking, having completely forgotten that Sebastian was sitting with me in the car in the back seat. I been looking outside the window vacantly, wanting to escape the reality yet trying to think of ways how to alter my reality.

"Yes, I am fine. Can you make travel arrangements for London as soon as possible?"

"The meeting didn't go that bad for you to escape the country. I thought it went pretty well, they are all on board with your strategy to buy out the automotive wing of Wilkinson Corporation and they were really enthusiastic to start a sports management part of our company."

"Oh don't be silly it's not that, I have to conduct business in London. And who says I am escaping on my own you are coming with me. I want you to oversee the deal to acquire the new club and eventually head our sports management department." He looks a bit confused, as he should be. To tell you the truth I don't think so I have got enough time to wait on the whole acquisition strategy of Wilkinson Corporation. I had some time to read the letter in the black envelope. Even though it didn't say much, but it said enough. Somehow the CIA has apprehended Natasha in Berlin and are keeping her captive somewhere, unless I give them all I have on my father. This doesn't make much sense, they have finally gone for the aggressive approach all too soon. To be honest, everything I have does not even come close to proving anything against my father, although it does against Mr Wilkinson. And if I do give them all I have, Wilkinson Corporation will be no more and I would not need any fancy strategies to grow our company but it might also put our company at risk. Either way, I need to get Natasha back, no matter what it takes. I have to be sure they are not bluffing; I need to know for myself. If they do have her, I don't know what they might have done to her. I guess it's pointless for me to ask how they know about her, I need to go find Berenger and know what is actually going on, his goons were supposed to keep a watch on her.

"Are you sure you are okay, Johann?"

"Seriously Sebastian stop worrying I am fine. Plan the journey for as soon as possible, tonight if possible."

"I will see what I can do."

Nothing of this makes sense right now, and I cannot think straight to make any sense of it at the moment anyway. I cannot let anything happen to her. I love her, I know I do. It might have taken an abduction by a government intelligence organization for me to realize that, but I know I do. I have loved her from the first moment I saw her and I cannot let anything happen to her. Nothing makes sense right now but even less will if something does happen to her.

"Johann, your private jet is already prepared for you to leave tonight."

"That was quick, good work." I need to find my calm, I cannot let him know what is going on.

"I didn't do anything, Gilbert did it for you. It was already arranged yesterday."

"Oh yes of course, I forgot I told him to do that. Thanks anyway, don't think so you would have enough time to pack your luggage, but to be honest shopping in London would not be that bad."

"Sounds like fun." Fun indeed, how the hell did Gilby know? Seriously what is going on?

"Welcome back, Johann. I was not expecting this visit if I am being honest, but I am glad to see you."

"It is good to see you too Colin. Can you try contacting Mr O'Brien and tell him I want to see him as soon as possible, preferably today?"

"I already did, he is on his way."

"Who is O'Brien, Johann?" How much do I want to reveal to you, Sebastian? The answer would be, nothing at all.

"Never mind that Sebastian. I would like you to meet one of my closest friend, Colin. Think of him as a Gilbert equivalent of London for me. Now, you have a very busy day up ahead. I would like you set up a meeting with the club and see how quickly we can come up to an agreement."

"Well, nice to meet you Mr Colin. I will do that Johann as a matter of urgency, I have already been informed that the FA has approved your bid to own a football club in England outright, whether it be as a personal acquisition or through the company."

"In that case I would like it as a company acquisition through our sports management wing. Make it happen."

"Certainly Johann, but I would really like to get some rest first. It was a rather long journey."

"Of course, Colin please show Sebastian to one of our spare rooms."

I need to find out what is going on, I cannot wait any longer. I am not really sure at this stage even if I want to reveal too much to Colin. I need to tread carefully. By now the CIA must know that I have travelled to Europe, and no matter the media façade behind this trip they would know why I have actually come here. I need to keep all my cards close to my chest.

"I believe Sebastian will be quite comfortable in the room I used to stay in."

"Good, thank you."

Colin comes back within few minutes, "Now that he is in the room and out of earshot, would you mind telling me what you are doing here?"

"I don't think so I can, Colin. I am not entirely sure myself."

"Love is a mysterious thing, makes you do what logic perceives not."

"What are you talking about Colin?"

"No need to play coy with me young master. Here take this." This is first time I notice he was holding a folder with presumable some documents that might explain how he knew I was actually here – I know Berenger would not have told him. I look confused, even though I know who these might be from, "What is this Colin?"

"A week ago, she came by and left this in my care and told me in case she gets taken hostage that I should hand them over to you. It might explain why she was being kept hostage against her will."

"How are you sure she has been taken hostage?"

"You coming over here is a sure sign. She and I both agreed that you were intoxicated by her, and grown a deep rooted love for her. And if you got to know something happened to her, that you would come for her rescue."

"It is not that simple, Colin."

"Johann, the feeling was mutual from her end as well. Time to stop bottling it up and take action." I go silent for a while. It gives me great joy to know that she feels so strongly about me as well, fills my whole body with ever-glowing warmth. But at the same time I am extremely scared for her and feel utterly helpless. I need to keep calm, this is why they have done it, to speed up the process, to make me lose focus, so I make a mistake. One wrong step and this can all blow out of proportion. "Johann, go through it. It will help you understand. I think so you are ready to know, no matter what my brother thinks, take it."

I take the folder to my room and sit it down on my desk. It feels heavy, there is a lot to go through in here. I sit myself down, wishing I had asked for a cup of coffee before I went to my room. Now it might feel slightly awkward going back and asking for one. Wait, no need to, there is a cup of coffee by my bedside table. I bring it over to my desk, take a sip, perfect temperature, and open the folder. There are various paper documents in here. Receipts, letters, communication memos, all dated way back to the time of the war. I spread them all out trying to make sense of them, they are from various different companies, companies who I thought had already packed it in. This doesn't make much sense, from the first look of it there seems to be a lot of fraudulent activities going around concerning Wilkinson Corporation, involving a bit of Blackmore Industries as well and affiliated very unknown to me subsidiaries. But it really doesn't explain why she would have given it to me. This is not what we were searching, if I wanted to know this I would have asked Sebastian. This doesn't make much sense. I topple over the folder just to see if there is anything else inside, and a compact disk falls out. Interesting, I take a sip of my coffee again, and light a cigarette, very interesting.

"I came around as fast as I could. I am extremely sorry Johann, but all my men are still hunting down the whereabouts in Berlin." I close the lid of my laptop and look at him. He doesn't just look slightly scared, he looks a bit sad. There seems to be a lot of mixed emotions going through his head, I need him focused, I need myself focused.

"How did you lose her?" I motion him to sit down; he chooses to sit by the corner of the bed, close to me by the desk. He is trying to compose himself; does he know what is on the CD?

"Natasha tracked down a lot of information which she chose not to share with me, instead with Colin. Is there anything in there that can help us find her?" Doesn't seem like she did, but I have a feeling he still does know what might be in it.

"I asked you a question Mr O'Brien, I expect you to answer it with acceptable explanation."

"I am sorry, Johann. We were keeping an eye on her from a distance as she was going about her investigations all across Europe. It is only till after she came to see Colin, that things got a bit complicated. Before she came here, she was in Berlin. I left 2 of my men behind in Berlin and we followed her to London, just me and Steve, the rest were trying to dig up few leads in Prague. They turned out to be dead ends, created to distract us. My men in Berlin got taken by CIA, and are probably held somewhere I do not know but possibly with Natasha. She knew we were keeping an eye on her and gave us the slip in London – that is when we lost her."

"I am sorry about your men, but I have an idea where she might be. There is an abandoned orphanage in Berlin. It is not a great building, so it's not that noticeable. I think they are holding them in there." He looks at me now, worried.

"We need to be careful then. You need to buy us some time."

"I will. I am flying back to the states tomorrow. I have set up a meet with the CIA to give them what they think they want, and what I couldn't care less for them to have. You have 48 hours to make this happen, their guard will be down. You need to get her out of there."

"I will." He takes this as a cue to get up and go on about however he will make this happen.

"Mr O'Brien, this cannot fail."

"I know. There is a lot more than your love riding on this. Your dad has fucked us all over." He leaves the room. He needs to get this done no matter what. Colin has been standing by the door, I believe throughout the entire conversation. He comes in and sits beside me where Berenger was sitting.

"Are you sure about the orphanage?"

"Yes. You have seen all that is on the CD, you know it makes sense. My mother had another child, a girl, Gladys, whom she gave away to the orphanage in Berlin. The same Gladys, was soon after adopted by a generous rich philanthropist, Marcus David Wilkinson, and renamed her Galadriel. No wonder she and my father are working together, the CIA knows this maybe they are all working together in a jumbled up orgy of crookedness. Natasha found this out which puts their entire operation in jeopardy, they have her there and I think they wanted me to know this."

"What about your father?"

"One CIA mind trick at a time, Colin."

---

I am standing here, in this damp forsaken place under the bridge holding these documents in my hands, lost and bereft of all feeling, daring not to act out of character but knowing that I might not have much control over myself. I cannot remain standing here in this filth, I cannot bear it anymore but at the same time I wish gravely to bury myself and the last remaining evidence of my negligent soul in this sewage ridden hell. I need to act fast, now that it has come down to it, I fear facing the truth – no not facing, just acknowledging it.

He must be held accountable, they all must be held accountable for playing their part in creating the nightmares of my world. I need to be careful, I know it has to be me to deliver my father's end to him, I just wish now it didn't had to be me although I had always wanted it to be me. The hesitation is not out of some misplaced love but it is the fear of association that haunts me. It grips my soul and drags me down to the depths of degradation, I begot from the very seed of deceit and evil that I wish to get rid of. I might play a vital role in riding the world of him but his blood through me would still survive – I am not ready to face that reality – I am not ready to face my own convictions.

Just a few years ago when I alarmed CIA of my suspicions, they did not take me that seriously. And then they approached me cautiously first and enabled me to seek their help, tried to persuade me that I am doing the right thing for the country and for the people. What a fool I have been made out of? They played me, like everyone else. They never wanted my father, he was always theirs to have, they wanted Marcus. They only wanted to make their hold even stronger, by making me his enemy and succeeding after him. Not a fatal enemy but a traditional enemy, who would eventually take control of the company only to lose all conscious control to them. There are no records showing my father's direct involvement in the Nazi Regime, the CIA must have erased them, it is as if he was never part of any shady misgivings. I hold with me the last slimmer of a proof about him, about his past, only to hand it over for them to be erased. Maybe in some sense, my father played for the greater good at start, being part of the American Intelligence even before its formal establishment, infiltrating the Nazi regime and helping to bring it down. But I think so he played both sides, they cannot expose him because it will expose them – but they do want him dead, and no matter what so do I. Marcus being my father's accomplice and not a direct CIA asset can be burned, and the burden of blame can entirely fall on him. But above all they want the CD from me, so they must know about Gladys being my sister – does it mean she is working with them or with my father.

The hidden Nazis and their hoard of gold and art uncovered by the CIA. The multi-billion dollar business transferred to public holdings to fund yet another secret invasion, in the name of whatever can fool everyone. And in all this, my father would be exposed as a war hero, who brought them victory from within, who probably sadly loses his life trying to be a hero one last time, saving the world from Marcus Wilkinson. Predictable and boring, not entirely far from the truth or the truth that I will help to make it happen.

I receive a text, 'We have her Johann, she is safe.' A tear drops my cheek, I have never been so relieved in my entire life.

"Ah Johann, you are early. I believe you have something for me." I turn around to see the slimy face I have grown to detest over the past few years. Agent Michael, there is just something wrong about him, always felt it. I cannot let him know that Berenger has found Natasha, they can still move on them if they wanted to.

"I am not giving you anything unless you give Natasha back to me." He smiles ever so slightly and then back to his pasty straight face again.

"Come now, we left her for your friends to pick up from the orphanage."

"You better not have hurt her." What an empty threat? What can I do if they had?

"We won't anymore …….. for now. I hope you know some good doctors." Now he is smiling, I have fallen into his trap of pulling my strings. I lung for him with my right fist, "you bastard!", he takes a step back and pulls out a gun and points at me.

"Temper, temper young raven, you don't want me to clip your wings do you." He is still smiling, while I am boiling with anger, I want to crush his skull with my bare hands.

"Hand over the documents and go play nurse with your broken girlfriend." I hand him the documents with gritted teeth, "I will find you one day Michael and make you pay for this insolence."

"Your mother thought the same, look where it got her. Killed by her own brother, such sweet tragedy." I look at him, slightly confused, still angry, confusion trying to take hold of it. "Don't look like a lost puppy, you need to have a nice talk with your Uncle Gilbert."

I ring Berenger as I walk away; he picks up on the first ring.

*"Is she alive?"*

*"Barely, but she is with the doctors now."*

*"How soon can you bring her to me?"*

*"Johann, she is not in a good state. You need to give her time to recover. And it's not safe for her over there right now, fix the shit over there first and I will get her to you."*

*"Okay."* An awkwardly long silence, I need to listen to her voice but for now I just need to trust him.

*"We just walked in Johann, there was no one. I don't really know what is going on, but what I do know that whatever has been started needs to be finished. And it would be best if you finish it, I do not pass judgement but I do like backing a definite victor."*

*"Very reassuring."*

*"Fix it, Johann."* And fix it I shall.

Fix it, what shall I fix? How many things are there for me to fix? I have been having passionate sex with my sister, who is actually working with my Nazi father as far as I know. Well I should say half-sister, her dad being my mother's lover - which makes it even worse. CIA has played me like a fool I am, got me to hand over everything I have over my father and also the proof that Gladys is my sister. I really don't know what is broken and what needs to be fixed. This has gone long enough, I need to find Gilbert. He is my uncle, my mother was murdered by him and CIA, and I been sleeping with my sister, my father is not really a Nazi but a CIA agent who eventually turned rouge but it's not really certain if he has or not, and again I have been sleeping with my sister. Did she know about it? Of course she knew about it, it makes sense since all my family is twisted and fucked up anyway. "What other surprises are there left for me?" I shout out loud.

"A lot more if you are willing to give an ear to them my dear Johann." I turn around to see Gilbert standing at the edge of my door. I guess my habit of talking to myself didn't really fix itself, what a waste of money and time that Dr Trent turned out to be. I turn my head back and ignore his presence. I do not know what to say to him, my emotions towards him are confused.

"I need to show you something – I think it is time for you to know. Maybe few years too late but you need to know now more than ever." I do not know why I still find it hard not to trust him. And to be fair he never really lied to me, I never asked him direct question about my mother and whether he killed her or not, or if he knows Galadriel is my half-sister. I follow him out of my room, down the stairs and into the main library, which is towards the back of our house. He goes towards the mantelpiece on the left corner gives it a bit of twist and a secret door in the floor opens up.

"Is there a bat cave underneath? Are you Batman, Gilbert?"

"I don't remember Batman being so handsome."

"Or such a treacherous jerk."

"Touché – Would you care to follow me to the Pohl-cave?"

I follow him down the winding dark stairs. It feels rank and smells of old memories, memories not belonging to me. The stairs lead into the middle of a room; it is too dark to make out anything. Gilbert reaches out and opens a switch to light the room. There are tables and chairs, maps with strange markings and bookshelves, and filing cabinets.

"What is this place?"

"This is where your mother and I planned and plotted to bring your father, Marcus and the CIA to justice."

"What do you mean you and my mother?"

"It was her idea."

"I don't believe you."

"Good, you have no reason to."

"Then why the fuck did you bring me here?"

"Because I need you to." He motions me to sit down, and I do it. This room has its own small kitchen area, it's a cosy little place. Actually there is a small toilet in here as well. This seems like an old nuclear bunker, this must have another way out as well. It makes sense for them to choose this place. No one goes to the main library, well my mother used to a lot now I know why. None of the servants are allowed in, because most books in here are collectibles and old, they need to be handled carefully. Only Gilbert tends to them, although I did recently notice him training one of our younger house staff on how to take care of these books. It is the perfect place to have this hideout. Gilbert goes towards the small kitchen counter, puts the kettle on to make coffee for both of us, probably coffee for me and tea for himself. I do not understand, they were all working together, if they suspected my father of going rogue why didn't they just alarm their superiors and had them deal with it, I am sure there would have been number of ways for it to be handled without anyone knowing anything about it. What is the fucking point of all of this? Gilbert comes back to the table and puts my coffee down in front of me. He sits himself down opposite to me, staring at his tea. Oh I feel a long monologue coming, kind of him to make me coffee before he starts it.

'Around thirty years ago, when your mum and I were about your age, we got our first assignment. Your mum was younger than me and Colin, I am guessing by this time you already know that she was my little sister, but she was very determined. While I got my first assignment by going through proper channels, taking a lot longer, MI6 fast tracked her progress. Our assignment was to monitor Blackmore and Wilkinson, and through them un-root the foundations of CIA. The British Intelligence has never trusted the CIA since its inception, and in more ways than one they have been proved right in their assumption. Your father was involved during the inception years of the CIA, and played a vital role in gathering information from within the Nazi regime, that helped all allies in defeating Hitler. Maybe because of this they turned a blind eye to his acquiring wealth during that time by illegal means. Wilkinson on the other hand was even trickier. He was an active member within the Nazi Regime, but somehow after the fallout was cleared of all wrongdoings of involvement, case put as classified since he was also an intelligence agent working undercover. We were to infiltrate the inner circle of Blackmore, Wilkinson and CIA by any means necessary. MI6 removed all records of your mother, Colin and I ever being related to each other. Your mother was given a new name, new identity actually complete new background originating from a small orphanage in Berlin. I have always been over protective of her, and it was hard for me to take, my dear Gladys becoming Klaudia.'

"Wait, my mother's name was Gladys? Same as Galadriel's actual name?"

"No Galadriel's actual name is Galadriel, she just likes being called Gladys. I have to say it is a bit of a coincidence." Gilbert seems eager to get back to his story, but I need a minute to process this. Natasha and I have been fooled once again; Galadriel is not really my sister. Natasha uncovered the MI6 cover up story for my mother. Was it just by coincidence that we assumed what should not have been assumed? Or was it made obvious for us to assume?

'As I was saying, our objective was to infiltrate the inner Nazi circle, whose ring leaders were believed to be Blackmore, Wilkinson and CIA itself. Blackmore was considered the safest bet as a way in to that circle. William, your father, was on a trip around Germany, where he *'accidentally'* met your mother in Frankfurt. They fell in love, or she made him fall in love with her. This was never the plan, even though it seemed the most obvious way in, but it was never the plan. I joined the CIA, and made my way through as a double agent. I will not go into detail of how I got into CIA, to be honest I don't even know fully how MI6 managed to do it and I am very sure information like that is classified beyond my pay grade. I was eventually assigned to an esteemed and highly distinguished CIA agent, William. By that time it had been at least two years since I saw your mother and the Intel I was getting all the time from Headquarters was, that she has stopped communicating, they feared she had gone rogue. It was a strange feeling, when I saw her after all that time with

William. I could not express true joy to see my sister, but I could not contain myself so I let a tear fall down my cheek and William asked, *'Why are you crying Agent Pohl?'* and I just told him that she reminded me of my little sister who died few years back.'

"So mum had been with him for two whole years without finding anything out?"

"No no, she had found a lot out, she actually made this place her investigation room. She just didn't feel it was safe to contact MI6 not till I came around."

'So that night your mother told me all the Intel she had gathered on Blackmore, Wilkinson and the CIA. As far as we were concerned our mission was accomplished. We had enough proof to establish the link. But your mother was pregnant with you at the time and it meant handling things a bit different. If we went back, MI6 would have her abort the baby, she was merely 8 weeks in the pregnancy. I didn't see much wrong with an abortion as well; she had her whole career ahead of her. But for some reason she thought there was something special inside of her and she wanted to keep you.'

My phone rings, "Yes?"

"Hello, Mr Blakemore it is me Sebastian."

"Is something wrong?"

"No everything is good, actually very good. I have begun negotiations and probably would be able to buy the club for a mere fraction of its actual worth."

"That's great work. Well done. I have a feeling there will be a lot of money in sports management in the future, perhaps 10 times more than now."

"I totally agree. I just wanted to call you and thank you for this opportunity. I was a bit hesitant at, knowing soccer, or should I say football, but not confident I knew enough. I really was not sure, but I can see now it is a huge opportunity you have given me, to grow a sports empire. I just don't know what to say."

"Sebastian, I chose you for a reason. No need to thank, just make us some money. Okay, I need to go now, I expect you to report back once the deal has been finalised."

"Of course, Mr Blakemore." I end the call and just stare at my phone. Few years back a lot of people could not have imagined that we would see an actual hand-held phone that fits in a normal hand, but look at this Motorola wonder now, what will the future hold. I turn to Gilbert, who I notice is looking at me a bit concerned.

"Are you telling me that if mum would have gone through with abortion, she would still be alive?"

"Johann, stop blaming yourself. You were only a foetus, it was her decision. Don't you go insulting her memory by playing with ifs and buts, she made that decision in good conscience and I for one think it was a good decision." I seemed to have stepped on a nerve.

'Anyway, little by little I gained William's trust and eventually I was permanently assigned to him. Your mother and I started digging up more, and the more we dug the more we found there wasn't much concrete evidence against your father. At one point I thought your mother was intentionally diverting our investigations away from your father to protect your future. But it turned out she wasn't far from the mark. The CIA – or should I say OSS seemingly had dabbled both ways before entering into the World War, but in the end decided to side with the allies. A fraction of their initial operatives went rogue and your father was key in rooting them out. That is why the CIA believed him when he vouched for Marcus. And that is exactly where my suspicions were rooted and I thought your mother was overlooking it on purpose.'

"You are confusing me Gilby, is my dickhead of a father involved in this or not."

'Patience was never your virtue. Johann, what I am trying to say is, at the start your father's intentions were good and he did right by his country. Even after he did a lot of good and his efforts helped the allies gained a lot of advantage over the Nazis. But his connection with Marcus raised suspicions. So it turned out, to the outside world your father was a national hero but in reality he has been working against the country and the CIA. Even now, it would seem that he is trying to uncover a major Nazi underground organization through Marcus, who he is using as an asset. But I have had my doubts from the start and I still think this was your father's plan all along. He is planning a Nazi revival with him as the leader of that filthy pack.'

"Marcus is dead."

"Exactly that solidifies my suspicions even more."

"Can you say suspicion few more time because I don't think you have said it enough?"

"Behave."

'Because Marcus is dead, although even the CIA seems unaware of it – the organization still hasn't disbanded that means it was your father all along.'

"What about Galadriel? And who killed my mother? And do you still work for CIA and MI6 then?"

'Galadriel is working for the CIA, they asked for her assistance same as yourself. But she has gone above and beyond of what was required of her although recently questions have arisen in my mind of her intense immersion into this. She has kept the death of her father a secret and Wilkinson Corporation has been run without the complete power of attorney transferring to her under the assumption that Marcus Wilkinson is still alive.'

"Why would she do that?"

"I do not know Johann. But she is under my care. I reached out to her on behalf of the CIA, she is my responsibility."

"So you are still working for both?"

'After the death of your mother, I ended communications with MI6. I had lost faith in both organizations. She made me a promise to look after you and that is what I dedicated myself to do no matter what the consequences. But recent events have pushed me to re-communicate with MI6. Obviously I had always maintained my cover with CIA, and it was a blessing in disguise when they asked me to be completely assigned to your father so I can look after his only son.'

"Why did the CIA asked me to look into my father then?"

'They knew you were trying to investigate matter, and the resources you had at your disposal meant it would be really hard to stop you. You were trying to find your mother's killer and they wanted to divert your attention by making you go after your father. They also wanted to destroy all evidence even remotely linking your father to anything Nazi, and now they have got it because of yours and Natasha's investigations.'

"Not everything."

"I am not surprised."

"So who killed my mother?"

'I killed your mother, Johann. I killed my sister, to keep the investigations and you alive. Your father found out that she was working for some other agency and reported it to CIA. They had to make it appear like an accident so they asked me to do it. Your mother saw this as the only way, to solidify my allegiance to the CIA and to save you from being a fugitive baby. We were backed into a corner and didn't think there was any other way out. We could not reveal MI6 being involved. So we made her appear as an FBI agent, trying to do internal investigation. She said to me, 'you live by the code, you die by the code', I should never have listened to her. Neither party would ever confirm any involvement. She didn't drown, I killed her. I held her in my arms under that lake till her last breath ran out. I killed my own sister.'

Gilbert starts crying hysterically. I want to console him, but I can't. He killed my mother, and all this time I was hunting for the murderer. I walk out of that room, leaving him crying by himself. I need some fresh air; I go out into the gardens, take out a smoke and light it. The first puff and it starts sinking in. My world has not been turned completely inside out, but it has certainly been twisted enough. I cannot wait anymore; this needs to be sorted now.

I have to end this, I cannot wait any longer, I have to end this now. One way or another I have to confront that monster, I do not care, I need to end this, I need to end him.

I go back in and walk towards the study – one of the many study/office rooms, whatever you want to classify them as, I have never cared to, mini libraries – in the house. This one is just as secluded as the one with the secret bunker. This is my father's main study, where no one can go, always locked. I never liked going in there because it reminded me of something that I could never remember. I copied the key for it ages ago, just never bothered going in there, but if there is going to be something it has to be in there that will give me a clue on how to proceed. As I walk in the study after unlocking the door, deceptively heavy doors, I start remembering a little. It doesn't always used to be locked up. I used to hide beside the mantelpiece just outside the study, adjacent to the room, I look back - it is still there. Funny how you forget such things. I used to hear my parents argue in full swing. I was afraid of the shouting – the excessive shouting – but it always ended in silence, long drawn out silence, which I hated even more. I used to wait and wait just to see if mum was fine, afraid to go in but always ready to save her if she needed to be saved. I usually used to fall asleep hiding besides it and then she would come out pick me up and put me to bed, with a good night kiss. Somehow I could sense the sadness yet deep affection in her kiss, reassured of her safety I would sleep deeply imagining myself a knight saving my queen from the evil monster. She always came out of that room, and after she passed away I never came near this room till I grew older only to find it locked, no shouting just dead silence, this fucking cursed room.

It reeks of whiskey and cigar in here – a combination that I do not necessarily detest, actually I love the combination just not when I think it is something he likes as well. The animal trophies he has in here, I abhor them, so much cruelty made glorious for the amusement of men, feeding their masculinity. I shall put his head up there once I am through with him. Where is he? Where is he hiding?

There are few papers lying on the chair by the fireplace. I go over, pick them up and sit down. He means to sell the mansion, so he knows and is running off to Argentina. Such a beautiful country shall not be made vile by his presence. I smell something, a scent I have grown familiar with recently but also a scent I can remember from years gone by. My mother used to wear this scent, and so does – Galadriel.

Where are they? Where are the scoundrels that plot a mischief? I get up in a fury not knowing what to think. I feel a draft – even the minutest of drafts can be felt in this dark and rank room. But this draft is freshening and slightly damp, coming from below rather than above. I look over at the fireplace and I see the smallest of gaps – a crack running all the way through, could it be this cliché?

I go over and give the fireplace a nudge from the side, lo and behold it moves a bit – I give a stronger nudge and it slides across giving way to a staircase going downwards. How many secret rooms does this mansion have? Naturally I go in.

I go down the stairs; it is a long way down. Luckily I have a torch in my pocket otherwise I would have to train myself to be a bat – don't really think sonar is my thing. This seems to run all the way through the manor – dark and damp. There is a door here in this long corridor – ordinary unmarked door. There is nothing ordinary about a door in a secret passageway. I open it, it's unlocked, maybe recently opened. Someone has gone through just not got back to lock it I guess, I am on the right path. I go in with caution, there is a light switch – I turn it on – and there is a mini armoury in here. Guns upon guns of so many kinds I do not even recognize. This is a closed room, so perhaps someone has taken something from it and not bothered locking it. Let's not pretend who I think that someone is. What is that old Cretan planning? I must find him. I take a handgun from the wall, where other more destructive weapons hang, I check for the magazine and load the gun – I will find some use for you.

I get out of the room and go further down the corridor. I must be below our gardens now, I have by my reckoning already walked the distance of the mansion, and the direction this underground passageway is curved, I should be below the extensive garden at the back. I don't suppose it is a passageway or a corridor it is a bloody tunnel. It runs long and deep, there is no flooring and the ground here is moist leaving footprints as I go. And now for the first time I notice two sets of footprints ahead of my own. At least two people have gone ahead of me. There are many other similar footprints going either side, but these two sets are more prominent, more recent. This tunnelled passageway, lets agree to call it that I cannot keep on calling it something else every time, is held up by wooden pillars steadied by concrete. I see more doors now, six with four on the right and two on the left. I try opening the first two on either side, but the both seemed locked. These are steel enforced doors, I cannot knock them down with brute force. Perhaps it's not the time to try to open them anyway. Looking at the footprints, they have only gone in two of these rooms and then they lead further ahead. I check the rooms where the footprints lead in and out, not locked, one of them is a study with historical books and detailed maps and the other is a food storage – food of long lasting sort. There is another room with a wooden door, its open. Sleeping quarters seem like, with bunk beds at least ten to sleep twenty people. It looks clean and kept well, but doesn't seem as anyone has slept here for a very long time. There are bits and pieces on the side of each bunk bed, combs, creams, radio, and a scarf on one. A personal army of some sort hiding and living here, maybe I should have taken more than just one gun. Seems like a nuclear war bunker, an extensive one. Lots of rich people have places like this built in their mansions after the scare of the cold war, but this is completely something else.

Not to mention this Mansion already has one where my mother made her office.

I must have been walking now for at least over 15 minutes and I have walking at a very fast pace. How long does it run? It seems never ending. As I see on the ground making sure I am still following the footsteps, the ground starts becoming a bit stony, like the edge of a cave. It seems to be coming to an end; actually as I look up ahead with the little light of my torch I see a wall – a stone wall. There is a switch on the side of the wall, which has a lightning bolt sign next to it and I notice for the first time a series of emergency lights running all the way back. There must have been a switch to light the tunnel at the start, anyway might as well that I didn't open it; don't want them to know I am following them. I see the faintest outline of a door, a door in the stone wall – half expecting it to have elvish ruins on it asking me to speak friend and enter. It is slightly ajar, must have been used recently as well, I open it carefully making sure not to make too much noise muttering 'Mellon' under my breath.

I nudge it open, slightly at first not expecting what to find and then it gives way. It is too dark, I can hardly see anything even with my torch. It is a cave, rather in between a cave. I can hear a stream running by somewhere close. This must be where the old rivers run by the stream where mum and I used to wonder towards sometimes, she always told me never to go towards the caves because they are dangerous. Well now I am inside that cave, I don't think it counts, I never went in I was already in these caves. There are a lot of places like this around our estate, this is the only one where I never went. I negotiate the slippery floor with caution till I start seeing some light, an opening of some sort. The small tunnelled passageway lead to a door, which opened inside a cave, and this small cave arch has opened up inside a larger cave opening. The stream running from outside into the cave's gaping mouth from where it probably goes in the belly of its mysterious sanctuary. And there I spot them, on the other side of the narrow stream, at the end of this cave. They are kissing each other with an unfamiliar passion – not just kissing they are fucking – naked on the stony ground of this accursed alcove in front of another cave door. The opening where I am is a bit above the ground, there is a small ladder, I do not care for the ladder and just jump down onto the little stones that stop me from slipping. I walk towards them trotting over the small stream – they still have not noticed me. I pull out the gun, pointing towards them, and

stand right above them and now they notice me –
bewildered – writhing in their compassionate sweat.

"Oh no, don't stop on my account. Carry on. I can always kill
you both when you finish fucking."

"Put that gun down, son." He gets up, bollocks naked, trying
to take control of the situation. While Galadriel looks at me,
unashamed yet thoughtfully.

"Son? Don't fucking call me that! You miserable piece of Nazi
shit."

"You got it all wrong."

"Oh I suppose you just slipped and fell into my bride to be
cocks up. No I got it just right, you slime – I got it just right.
Get up you whore." She gets up without making any remarks.

The door behind them seems of some importance. I make
them open it and walk inside with me following behind –
naked they came into this world and naked they shall depart
it, drowning in their blood.

"What is this place?" There is a switch on the wall next to the
door I open it. I look around and all I can see is various sized
things half-wrapped up in cloth. They seem like paintings,
gold ornaments glittering and huge trunks which for obvious
reasons I don't know what they hold.

"Just a warehouse, at least let me put my clothes on."
Galadriel interjects my investigative glances.

"You feeling a bit cold are you? Shut the fuck up. Both of you, on your knees right now." They both go on their knees side my side.

"You can have all of this, it is yours by right my son."

"I told you to stop calling me that, you sick son of a bitch. By right it belongs to the ashes of all those you killed in the camps, you vile beast."

"O' no no …."

"O' yes yes, don't even try to wriggle your way out of this you old shit. But you, my sweetheart, my dirty little whore – I knew your father was his accomplice but I had no idea that you were even worse than him. I didn't want to have that idea."

"You are such a whiny little petulant boy. For all your nosing around you know fuck all. My father has been on death's door for over a decade now. And no before you say it I am not your half-sister, that rouse was just to keep your other little whore busy, shame she still breathes."

"I thought I told you to shut up." Weird coincidence, a very weird coincidence that she would think about creating a story about her being my sister, have Natasha follow and then we end up uncovering that it is also a story my mum created of her past in the same orphanage – but she has no idea – I don't know if I have any idea.

"I have had enough of this." He gets up, trying to test his bravery against mine. I can see he wants to walk towards me and take my gun, but he is hesitant.

"Have you now?"

"Yes, who do you think killed your mother? You have always been such a stupid boy – she should have taken you with her to the grave. Gilbert should have just killed both of you."

Bang! His brains blasted – a clean shot and he falls with an undignified heavy thud next to Galadriel, she looks over in horror. I look behind me and I see Gilbert holding a gun with relief on his face – he probably wanted to do this for a very long time.

"Johann I ….."

"I know you had to Gilby – your sister, my mother – there was no other choice. And I know you have had to live with it for so long, it is all right, I do not put any blame on you."

"Thank you."

"No thank you. For all he has done I still didn't think I could pull the trigger."

Galadriel is still looking at my father's body with absolute horror, his blood is forming a pool around her – that look is not of love but lost opportunity. Gilbert puts his gun away and looks at me. "You have to make the decision now."

"I know and I have." Galadriel looks at me – her beautiful body shivering with fear and cold, legs and that sumptuously rounded ass socked in my father's blood. Even now I find it hard not to lust for her.

"My father and Wilkinson clearly were tied together in this. She thinks no one knows the whereabouts of her father, but she couldn't be more wrong. Berenger and his men have recovered him from Argentina – they will be bringing him here in a while. Well when I say him, I mean his corpse, he did die but his body is fresh enough. You will move all of this hoard with them into the Wilkinson Manor. You and my father will 'kill' him there in an attempt to capture him. You obviously will get injured in the process and my father will get a bullet to his head, Berenger will make sure there are enough bodies to stage the scene of a shootout. You will take your time in notifying CIA, unexplained time lapse can be a bit beneficial. The mention of my father from most documents have already been removed by the CIA themselves, they don't know that he was going to betray them even further. Both of you will be hailed as the best of agents, probably get some secret medals as well. You can then report back to MI6 telling them that it wasn't my father after all, it was all Wilkinson's doings. And this mystery will be solved once and for all with no evidence being left behind, leaving me and my company in peace. And hopefully you can find your peace in some way back in England."

"You intend to make this swine of a father of yours a hero?"

"I intend to absolve my involvement. I intend to live and not let him drag me with him. If it means him getting a hero's funeral, so be it."

"And what about her? You know she is not your sister, Johann."

"Neither is she my fiancée nor ever be my bride."

"She is my care Johann, she might have gone way of course but she is still my care, my asset."

I look at her once again with slightly more compassion than I did before.

"She went a bit too far I know. But she is not involved with this. She had the same intention as you, perhaps even more. She didn't want any of her father's money or inheritance; she just wanted to disclose his true self to the world. I do not believe her intention was to hurt you."

Gilbert takes his jacket and puts it over her. She says nothing but now I can see the shame on her face betwixt with anger.

"A lot depends on her testimony then?"

"She is my care Johann, I told you that."

"But she is not mine."

Bang! This time I pull the trigger, bullet straight through her head, all those practice hours actually paid off. She drops on the ground face forward, that's going to leave a mark.

"Johann .."

"You live by the code, you die by the code."

"But…."

"Change of plan; you, my father and Galadriel will go to the Wilkinson Manor to accomplish the deed."

"What have you done?"

"Just make it happen, Berenger and his men should be here soon. They might need further coordinates to locate this place, they will contact you."

It has been more than half a year and the only real goodbye I had with Gilbert was at that cave. Not really a goodbye just a witness to a cold blooded murder and a cover up. All those years, all the thoughts exchanged and that is how my relationship ended with my only true family. Of course we met briefly at the funeral, just a glance and an acknowledgement that perhaps it is best to part ways.

"What are you thinking about, Johann?" Natasha comes back from the shower with only a towel wrapped around her head, letting her body dry in the warmth of the fireplace. Few speckles of water, running down her, caressing her body, relishing her touch while I enjoy the spectacle. Her scars glisten in the low light of the room from the fire crackling the wood. Scars, so many of them – the sacrifice she gave to know the truth – yet what is the truth but another lie to mask the reality that haunts us all.

And what is it that she found out? Not much, just enough to stop her searching for it. Her mother was German, like mine pretended to be, her suspicions were not ill founded, a German jew, killed because of an association with my father, but there were others, so many others and her mother was just one of them herded for senseless slaughter. Her father was not jewish but he later became a Nazi who turned his own wife in to gain some extra points in the regime.

The letter my mother left me in Gilbert's care, I still have not dared to open it. He gave me at the funeral, didn't say a word then as well. But I believe it is time to open it and say my last farewell, I have in some way avenged her death. I open it, it is not much of a letter but a note, a long note.

*'Johann my sweet boy. I hope this letter finds you away from the evils of your father and in good health. I kept a lot of secrets from you; secrets that I dearly wanted to tell you but did not know how to tell you. If you are reading this, that means I never found a way to tell you, and I am long gone. Know that no matter what happened to me it was not your mistake, you were the only thing in my life worth living till I did. But there is one more, one more piece of my heart that I left behind because I had no other choice.*

*It seems easier to write about this than talk to you about it, but I hope you have grown and matured enough to understand this. Your father is a Nazi who helped build and operate Office of Strategic Services and later on shaped the foundations of the Central Intelligence Agency. I was a spy, an operative working for MI6. Gilbert is your uncle, he might seem a bit stern but he is the most caring person you can ever meet. And Colin I hope you get to meet one day, is my little brother, a sweet heart. Gilbert, Colin and I were all that was left of the Pohl family – a lot had been taken from us and at least Gilbert and I were determined to take revenge, Jews or not Germany was still our home and we wanted to make those monsters pay for what they did to all of us. I hope you have already figured all of this out or Gilbert has finally managed to tell you the truth and everything is well behind you. But like I said there is another who was not as fortunate as you to have anyone around – I don't know maybe that might have turned out to be a fortunate thing for her. Your father used to let me go on holiday trips in the early years with you, you were only 2 back then and he didn't suspect anything of me back then. I never wanted to make it obvious and go to England or Germany so I used to go to the beautiful city of Antalya. I do not know if you remember but you used to have so much fun on the beach. I met her father there on my first visit; he was this handsome man who used to run a local English bookstore. He had the books of the most unknown authors. He was so amazing in the way that he had no secrets to hide; he was not pretending to be a bookstore owner - that was him. We spent hours and hours talking to each other, and obviously one thing led to another. I want you to know that it was love, I don't want you to think anything less of your mother – it was pure and honest love. For two years I went to Antalya every chance that I could get to spend time with Baran, until the last time when Marcus found out about us. I never saw Baran again – but I bargained my life and dignity for his. I am not sure if he let him go, but I had to try. Few weeks after I found out that I was pregnant – I panicked. I didn't know whose was it, all I knew it wasn't your father's. I turned to Marcus for help; well I had the upper hand to blackmail him. He thought it was his, after what he had done to me and so I let him believe it. He convinced your father that I was going through some troubling time and might be better for me to stay in a secluded environment in Berlin, under supervision obviously. Your father was already knee deep with his whores, he couldn't care less. So that was that, and I gave birth to your sister in Berlin, and sadly gave her up in an orphanage. Your father had no idea about it and all Marcus knows was that the girl died at birth, never survived. That was the only way to keep her safe.*

*Her name is Natasha, and she is your sister. If she is still alive, take care of her, you must find her. She is a child born of a happy memory and she doesn't deserve to be left all alone.'*

I am reading the note, with trembling hands. She goes on about the details of the orphanage in Berlin and perhaps I should start searching for her over there. Tells me about birth marks and what not, and again and again begs me to find her and look after her. I look up at her, Natasha, my sister, naked, drying her hair. This cannot be, maybe this is another fabrication of Galadriel to screw up with my mind planted before I killed her. I never read it so I never asked her. No I have done too much to get some happiness in my life, this cannot be. But Galadriel planted evidence to make me think that she was my sister as a fail-safe policy so we never get married but still get what she wanted, full control over both companies after she had killed me. Gilbert never saw that, but I guessed it. She never said anything about Natasha. This all adds up, the missing story of my mother. No, no it cannot be, I do not want it to be.

Natasha comes closer and gives me a kiss, looks me in the eyes, "What are you thinking about?"

"Nothing, just thinking how lucky I am to have a wonderful girl like you in my life – who if all goes to plan will be married to me."

"Liar. Is that your mother's letter?"

"Yes."

"Can I read it?"

I get out of bed and walk towards the fireplace and throw the letter in the flames. "I am done lingering on old memories; I wish to make new ones with you." She just looks at me and gives me a smile, a smile a bit too familiar to me.

Life is what we make of it, and I make it to be mine to control and do as I will. It is time to burn the past – no one has any use of the past.

# About the Author

**Momus Najmi** writes stories in multiple genres, and also likes to dabble a bit in poetry from time to time. 'The Silent Betrayal' is his debut novel.

He is an ardent atheist and humanist, and a passionate advocate of logic and reason in life. Over the years he has developed a deeper sense of egalitarianism and promotes it at every appropriate opportunity. He wishes to explore the abstract realities of human mind, the absurdness of our existence within the universal existence.

---

If you wish to keep an eye out for any future work by him, he can be followed via:

**Website:** www.momusnajmi.net

**Twitter:** @theworldofmomus

---

Printed in Poland
by Amazon Fulfillment
Poland Sp. z o.o., Wrocław